LOSING CONTROL

The Control Duet

Book 1

LINDSEY POWELL

Books by Lindsey Powell

The Perfect Series

Perfect Stranger

Perfect Memories

Perfect Disaster

Perfect Beginnings

The Complete Perfect Series

Part of Me Series

Part of Me

Part of You

Part of Us

Part of Me: Complete Series

Control Duet

Losing Control

Taking Control

Games We Play Series

Checkmate

Poker Face

Dark Roulette

A Valentine Christmas

End Game: A Valentine Wedding

Games We Play: Complete Series

Wreck My Heart Series

Wrecking Ball

The Untouchable Brother

A note from the author

A note from the author

*** Trigger warning ***
This story is intended for readers 18 years and over due to scenes of domestic abuse and violence.

Prologue

I remember the first hit as if it were yesterday.

The first time that his hand connected with my cheek.

The first time that he caused me physical pain.

The first time that he shattered my already fragile heart.

He preyed on my vulnerability. He took my confidence away from me. He ruined my perfect ideas of a loving relationship.

I let him control me.

I let him abuse me.

I let him break me.

I don't want to be this person.

I don't want to be weak.

I need to save myself, but to do that, I must understand why.

Why did I let him dictate?

Why did I let him hurt me?

Why did I lose control?

Chapter One

AT FIRST GLANCE

His eyes met mine from across the room, and his smile made me go weak at the knees. I thought that he was looking at someone stood behind me, and I even turned around to check, but there was no one there. My friend, Kim, told me a few weeks ago that he fancied me, but I just laughed at her.

Why would he fancy me? I mean, there is nothing special about me.

I had just gotten out of an unhappy relationship, I was sleeping on Kim's sofa as I had no home of my own, and I was working as an office temp. My appearance had become a little gaunt over time, due to the relationship that I had just come out of, and I hadn't made an effort with my looks for months.

My long, blond hair was limp, my skin had paled, my cheeks had become hollow, and I had lost my curves that I used to love so much. But more soul-crushing than that were my eyes. My once bright, vibrant, full of life baby blues were now dull and lifeless. You could tell a lot from someone's eyes, and every morning when I looked in the mirror, I was ashamed of what I had become.

A shadow of my former self.

A recluse.

A fucking heartbroken mess.

I couldn't even call myself a hot mess. I had kept the 'mess' part and dropped the 'hot.'

I used to be able to command a room, have men's eyes following me as I sashayed past them, knowing how good I looked.

It's amazing how one earth-shattering revelation can destroy you and make you become someone that you despise.

"Lucy," I hear Kim say loudly, disrupting me from my thoughts. I turn to look at her, my gorgeous brunette-haired, green-eyed best friend. She is the total opposite of me. She radiates beauty, shines like a beacon, and gives you a warm fuzzy feeling inside.

We've been friends for years, and I thank God every day that she is in my life.

Kim is sat at her desk, which just so happens to be next to mine.

"What?" I reply, quieter than she was in saying my name.

"Finally, she listens," Kim says in a sarcastic tone. "That's the third time that I have called your name in the last few minutes."

"Sorry," I reply as I chew on the end of my pen.

"What the hell were you thinking about? Or should I say *who* were you thinking about?" I watch as her eyes glance over to the same place mine were a few minutes ago. Kim giggles as I feel the blush start to creep across my cheeks.

"I wasn't thinking about anything, or anyone, in particular," I respond, trying to sound innocent but failing miserably.

"Mmhmm."

"I wasn't," I insist.

"Lucy, you don't need to pretend with me. I have known you since the age of fourteen, and I know when you are lying," she says as the corners of her mouth threaten to pull into a smile.

"Okay, fine," I admit, conceding defeat. She always has been able to read me like a goddamn book.

"Why don't you just ask him out?" she asks, as if it would be no big deal.

"No way!" I say a little too loudly.

Miriam, sat at the desk to the right of me, looks over and tuts loudly. I give her an apologetic look whilst Kim just glares at her.

Kim isn't one to take notice of what Miriam thinks, seeing as she is well known for being the office busybody. If you want to know anything about anyone in this office, then you just go to Miriam for the details.

"You need to grow some balls," Kim says, her attention firmly back on me.

"No thanks, I am perfectly fine as I am."

"Oh, come on, Luce," she says, exasperation creeping into her tone. "You have been single since Tom left you nearly six months ago. You need to get out there and have some fun."

I grimace slightly at her words.

Has it really been six months? It feels like weeks rather than half a year.

"Kim, it's not that easy." This is my usual pathetic answer, and one that I swear has been programmed into me, seeing as I have used it for what feels like the millionth time.

I thought that Tom was the love of my life, my reason to breathe, my happy ever after. Of course, those illusions were shattered when he went and cheated on me with one of my closest friends. Not that she is a close friend anymore. I can't even bring myself to say her name.

"Look, I know how much Tom hurt you, but you have to let it go."

"Easy for you to say," I reply, a little too harshly and unfairly. It's not Kim's fault that I am in this shitty phase in my life.

Kim has been in a relationship with Jeremy for two years, and they are happily engaged. Jeremy was in the same class as us at school, and the three of us have always been friends. It wasn't until Kim and Jeremy were twenty-five that they finally gave in to how they felt about one another. Together, they have the perfect partnership, and I am so happy for them, even if my mood right now doesn't show it.

I feel Kim's eyes glaring at me, and I start to feel guilty about my comment.

"Sorry," I say with a sigh.

"It's okay," she says with a flick of her wrist. "I was there, remember? I saw how his and Carley's betrayal broke you."

I physically cringe as Kim says her name.

"I don't want to talk about her," I reply sharply.

"It was his fault too, Luce."

"I know that, but she was supposed to be my friend, and she stabbed me in the back in the worst way possible."

I need to be free of this pain that crushes my soul every day. I deserve more than this. I deserve to be loved, worshipped, and treated like a queen.

My heart aches, and I miss my friend, Cal. Cal Bailey, a man who would never so much as give his girl a dirty look, let alone cheat on her. He left to go travelling months ago, and there isn't a day that goes by that I don't fiercely miss him.

I wish that he hadn't gone, I wish that he were here to give me a hug and tell me that everything is going to be okay. But he isn't. I have to do this on my own, when I'm at my weakest and feeling more vulnerable than ever before.

My hurt over Tom and Carley isn't going away. It should be going away by now, but it isn't, and I have no idea how to make it better.

I hear Kim sigh, and I sneak a look at her out of the corner of my eye. She gives a little shake of her head and returns to her work. She's probably sick to death of carrying my miserable arse around with her, and hey, who could blame her? There is only so much anyone can take, but I hope to God that she has more patience left within her, because I couldn't have gotten through the last six months without her.

As I focus back on the figures on the computer screen, I allow my mind to take me back to that awful moment when I walked in on Tom and Carley fucking, in mine and Tom's bed. The sight of my friend laid on her back with Tom on top of her will forever be ingrained in my mind. Tom's arse bobbing up and down. Carley's face showing just how much she was enjoying his dick up inside of her.

I squeeze my eyes shut, begging the image to fuck off out of my head. I don't need to keep reliving it. I don't need to stay in the goddamn past.

Carley, a friend for six years, who turned out to be an enemy.

Tom, my boyfriend for two years, who turned out to be a complete arsehole.

My desk phone rings, breaking me from the unwelcome images flooding my mind. I shake my head and pick up the phone, putting on a polite voice as I speak.

I feel a tingle creep its way up my spine, and my eyes dart up to see the handsome man across the room staring at me. I bite my lip to stop myself from smiling, and I lower my head to hide the fact that I am blushing.

I don't need another man in my life.

All they do is cause trouble, and I've had more than enough of that to last me a lifetime.

Chapter Two

THE FIRST INTERACTION

I turn off my computer and gather my belongings together as I get ready to leave the office.

"Hey, Lucy," I hear a voice say, making me jump.

I was so busy putting my things into my handbag that I failed to see Michael walking over to my desk. The very handsome Michael who just so happens to have caught me looking at him more than once today.

Michael Chandler. Office sex God. Brown eyes that are the colour of dark chocolate. Light brown hair that has been styled to give that casual, sweeping look. Tall, with a fairly firm body from what I can see with his tight-fitting shirt on.

"Oh, hi," I say, shyness creeping into my tone and taking over. I feel myself blush as his heated gaze is fixed firmly on me.

Christ alive, Lucy, stop blushing.

"Sorry, I didn't mean to make you jump," he says, flashing me his gorgeous smile. His eyes sparkle, much like they did earlier when he was staring at me from across the room. "Listen," he continues. "I hope that you don't think that I am being too forward, but I was wondering if you would like to go for a drink sometime?"

"Me?" I squeak, my eyes widening in surprise. He chuckles, and the noise alone makes my stomach flutter.

"Yes, you."

"Me and you?" I want the ground to swallow me up from my ridiculous response.

Stop acting like a bloody idiot, Lucy. A gorgeous man is asking you out, and you're asking daft questions.

"She would love to go," I hear Kim say from beside me. I turn my head to look at her, utterly shocked that she has just answered for me.

"She would?" I manage to say to her.

"Yes," she replies with a stern look.

Michael clears his throat, reminding me that he is still stood there. *Dear God, please let the ground swallow me whole, now.*

"How about Friday night after work?" he suggests. He's looking at me, but once again Kim answers his question.

"Perfect," she says with a smirk on her face. If she wasn't such a good friend to me then I might have been more than a little tempted to reach across and slap her.

"Great. Will I actually be able to talk directly to her when we go for a drink?" Michael asks Kim. I have no idea what shade of red I have gone, but my money is on a deep crimson.

"Of course," Kim replies, completely unfazed by my flustered state.

"I am still here you know," I say, managing to get my voice to work.

Kim has the decency to shut her mouth at this point.

"I look forward to it," Michael says as he starts to walk away from my desk.

"Okay," I answer feebly as I watch his retreating back leave through the office doors.

Once he is out of sight, I turn to Kim. She is smiling at me, mischief twinkling in her eyes.

"Kimberley Jenkins, how dare you," I scold her.

"What?" she replies, feigning ignorance.

"You know damn well what. Why did you just agree for me to go on a date with Michael?"

"Because he's hot, he's single, you're hot and you're also single. You like him, and he likes you. Why wouldn't you want to go out with him?" She makes a good point, but I'm still not over what Tom did to me.

"Kim," I say on a sigh.

"Look, you're only going out for a drink. This isn't a commitment of marriage or anything. It's just one drink, Luce."

"But what if it makes things awkward?"

"Awkward how?"

"I work with the guy. How awkward would it be if the drink didn't go well?" Nerves start to bubble up within me.

"If that happens then you just suck it up and get on with it," Kim says with a shrug of her shoulders.

"Oh, jeez, thanks for the advice," I say as I pick up my handbag and stand up. Kim links her arm through mine and we start to walk out of the office.

"Just have a little faith, Luce."

"Hmmm," I mumble.

I have been severely lacking in the faith department for months now.

Maybe Michael will be the one to bring it back for me?

Chapter Three

THE FIRST DATE

The last couple of days have dragged by as I have become more and more nervous about my date with Michael. It is now Friday, and the clock reads five thirty. Clocking off time, which means that Michael is about to pack his stuff up and walk over here, to take me on our date.

I make myself look busy, tidying my desk, faffing with my handbag, feeling more than a little flustered at the prospect of spending the evening with a man that isn't Tom. A man that totally knocks spots off of most others in the room. A man that I know will conquer my heart if I let him in. A man that is making his way over to my desk right this very second.

We haven't spoken much since he asked me out two days ago, but then I have been busy attending meetings and dealing with client complaints. Sometimes I wonder why I ever chose a job in marketing. All day long I deal with other people's problems. God forbid they actually listen to me—I mean, what the fuck do I know, what with my marketing degree and my general experience of all things advertising?

"Hey, Lucy, you ready to get out of here?" Michael asks as he comes to a stop in front of my desk.

"Uh… Sure." *Great start, Luce. I'm sure he didn't sign up for a date with a mumbling wreck.*

I pick my handbag up and make my legs push me off of my chair and into a standing position. I struggle to stop my hands from shaking, so I fold my arms across my chest.

"Have fun you two," Kim says, smiling away to herself.

"Thanks," I respond as I continue to move my legs forward.

Michael comes to the side of me and his arm brushes against mine. I feel a tingle run through me. *Keep it together, Lucy. You have to see this guy at work, don't make a fool of yourself.*

"I thought that we could go to Alan's," Michael says, referring to the local 'up-market' bistro that is just around the corner from our office.

"Okay." Thank goodness I decided to wear my smart, black pencil dress today. At least I am dressed appropriately. I give Kim a little wave as she excitedly bounces up and down on her chair. God, she's like a kid that's just been told they are going to Disneyland to fulfil all their childhood dreams.

We leave the office and walk in silence to Alan's as the tension radiates off of me. If Michael picks up on it, he doesn't say anything, which I am grateful for. He exudes no such tension. He has always come across as confident, which only threatens to intimidate me.

"After you," Michael says as he opens the door to Alan's for me. I thank him and then we make our way over to the bar. "Did you want to get some food, or just a drink for now?" he asks me.

"Just a drink is fine." I don't think I could eat even if I wanted to.

"Wine?"

"White, please."

I wait whilst Michael orders the drinks, my arms still folded across my chest. Alan's is already busy with people coming here for drinks at the end of their working week. I don't spot anyone from our office yet, which isn't a bad thing. I would rather this date be kept hidden from the prying eyes of our colleagues, especially

Miriam. She would be a fucking nightmare if she were to get wind of mine and Michael's little outing.

When our drinks are ready, Michael picks them up and leads me over to a secluded table for two in the far corner of the room. I take a seat opposite him and cross my legs, pleased with his choice of table. Here in the corner, I can keep myself in my little bubble.

I keep my back straight as I pick up my wine and take a sip. The cool liquid glides down my throat, and I hope that it does something to help calm me down.

"So, Lucy," Michael begins as he places his beer bottle on the table. "I finally get the chance to speak to you on your own."

"Uh, yeah. Sorry about Kim the other day. She gets a bit carried away." I try to sound as casual as possible, but even I can hear the slight wobble in my voice.

"I can tell," he replies with a chuckle. "You don't need to be so nervous… I don't bite." His smile relaxes me slightly.

"I'm sorry, I just haven't been out on a date for a while."

"A date?" he questions.

Oh shit. Have I read this wrong? Is this not a date? Is it just a friendly drink between co-workers?

"Relax, I'm joking," he says as he registers the panic on my face. I let out a nervous giggle as relief washes over me that I haven't read this situation wrong. "I've actually been wanting to ask you out for a while now."

"Really?" I ask, gobsmacked.

"Yeah, but I wasn't sure how long to leave it after you and Tom split up."

I feel the familiar emotion of sadness grip me on the inside and swallow down the lump that has formed in my throat. I wasn't aware that he even knew about Tom.

"Um…." No words come to mind as I battle to quell the discomfort rising within me.

"I apologise. I shouldn't have brought it up," he says with his hands held up in front of him. "It's just that, you know, the office grapevine likes to talk. News travels fast, and half of the time you don't know whether it's true or not." He has a genuine look of concern on his face, and I instantly feel stupid for my reaction.

Tom is gone, Lucy, but Michael is sat right in front of you.

Michael isn't Tom.

"It's okay," I say, finding my voice again. "It's been six months since we split up, so I shouldn't let it affect me."

"Hey," he says, reaching for my hand and placing his on top of mine. The simple gesture has me looking at him, straight into his dark chocolate eyes. "You don't have to explain yourself. Break-ups are hard, no matter how they occurred."

I smile softly at him. I never realised that he was this sweet.

I study his handsome face and I realise that I can either let what happened with Tom eat away at me, or I can move on and see where this thing with Michael takes me.

I opt for the latter.

I owe myself the opportunity to be happy.

Michael wants to get to know me, and I would be a fool to throw that chance away.

Chapter Four

A BUDDING RELATIONSHIP

"So," Kim says as we sit at our desks and eat our lunch. "Things seem to be going well with you and Michael."

"Mmmhmm," I mumble through a mouthful of salad. I may have a mouthful of food, but it doesn't stop the smile spreading across my face at the mention of Michael.

"Three dates in total," Kim continues with a raise of her eyebrows. She is fishing for information. "And is date number four happening anytime soon?"

I may be staying at Kim's place for now, but I don't feel the need to tell her about every aspect of my life. Plus, she has had the last couple of days off of work and has been staying at Jeremy's, so her snooping has been somewhat limited to the odd text message.

"It is," I reply coyly. I can feel the impatience coming off of her in waves as I fight to control the laughter that is threatening to break free from me.

"Lucy Fields, will you stop being so bloody secretive."

"I'm not," I say, feigning ignorance.

"Bollocks. Are you going to keep me guessing or are you just going to tell me what the deal is between you and Michael?"

I chuckle and decide to put her out of her misery.

"Date four is tonight, and all is going well."

"Well? Is that it?" she asks incredulously.

"Okay, it's going brilliantly."

"And have you… you know?" she says with a twinkle in her eye.

"Not yet," I reply, catching on to her implication straight away.

"Why not?" she says, her face pulling into a frown.

"Because we're taking it slow."

I don't want to rush things. Although I vowed to let myself be happy, I can't help myself from being a little bit cautious.

Kim opens her mouth to speak again, but the office doors open and Michael walks in. Butterflies rear up within me, and I wipe my mouth with a tissue to make sure that there is no salad dressing there.

"Ladies," Michael says as he comes to a stop in front of my desk.

"Hi," I reply, my heartbeat ratcheting up a few notches at his close proximity. My eyes appreciate his manly form in his navy-blue suit. His hair looks slightly ruffled, clearly from where he has just been outside in the wind.

"Michael," Kim acknowledges him with a nod of her head. He nods back at her before turning his attention to me.

"We still on for tonight?" he asks me as he puts his hands in his trouser pockets. His stance is commanding, and I feel a little tingle between my legs.

"Yeah, I'm looking forward to it."

"Good. I thought that we could go to my place and I would cook for us."

"Oh." I am caught off guard at the mention of his place. I just thought that we would be going for a drink like we have done on the other three occasions that we have been out together.

"We don't have to if you don't want to," he says, clearly reading my surprise.

"No, no. Going to yours is fine." I don't want him to think that I am uncomfortable with going to his place. Things are going so good between us, and I promised myself that I wouldn't allow my anxiety over what Tom did to me fuck this up.

The smile he gives me makes me want to run my lips over his.

Bloody hell, Lucy, take it easy. You wanted to take things slow just now, don't run before you can walk.

"Great." His reply is paired with a great big shit-eating grin, and it makes me feel all warm and fuzzy inside. "Well, I best get back to work," he says as more workers start to file back into the office, their lunch breaks over. He winks at me before walking across to the other side of the room and taking a seat at his desk.

"Dinner my arse," I hear Kim mutter from beside me.

"What was that?" I say as I pull myself out of my lust-filled haze.

"There is no way that you two are just having dinner. Did you see the way that he looked at you?"

"How do you mean?" I have no clue where she is going with this.

"Oh, please, he looks like he wants to strip you naked right here, right now."

"No he doesn't," I protest.

"Yes, he does, Luce. I'm telling you that tonight is the night that you finally get some much-needed action."

Chapter Five

A LITTLE DEEPER

As the working day draws to a close, I am a bundle of nerves, yet again. After what Kim said earlier, my mind has been a jumble of thoughts.

Is Michael really expecting me to sleep with him?

Am I overreacting?

Should I just throw caution to the wind if he tries to take things further?

I say goodbye to Kim as the questions whirl around my head. I take a few deep breaths as I walk towards the office doors, pushing them open to see Michael waiting for me on the other side.

"You ready to get out of here?" he asks me, that grin I like so much gracing his face.

I nod and am shocked to feel his hand grab mine, his fingers linking us together. My eyes immediately look around the hallway to see if anyone has noticed, which they haven't as they are all too busy scuttling out of here to go home.

My eyes shift to Michael, and he has the warmest smile on his face. The softness in his eyes releases some of my tension.

We're just a man and a woman getting to know one another.

It's a perfectly normal, everyday thing.

I just need to relax and allow myself to live.

He opens the door and leads me out of the building. Michael has already told me that he only lives a short walk away from here.

"I am so glad that it's Friday," he says, breaking the silence.

"Hard day?" I ask, enjoying the feel of my fingers still being entwined with his.

"Just pain-in-the-arse clients."

"Tell me about it." I can't help but roll my eyes. "My afternoon consisted of me trying to appease an existing client over an advert that she kept saying just 'wasn't right' but she couldn't explain to me why she felt this way. I sometimes wonder why I ever decided to work in a customer service setting," I say with a chuckle.

"Well, I'm glad that you did, because if you hadn't, then I may never have had the chance to meet you." His honesty shocks me, but I am saved from giving a response as he then announces that we have arrived at his place.

I look at the building to the right of me, and I am surprised to see that he lives in a block of run-down apartments. I am not a snob by any means, but I am well aware that this is one of the roughest areas to live in. It's not where I would have imagined he would live.

He pushes open the communal door and leads me up two flights of stairs. The faint aroma of urine reaches my nostrils, and I can't help but screw my nose up. Luckily, Michael is in front of me, so he doesn't see the look on my face.

We stop outside a red door with the number thirteen on it. I have to stop myself from laughing at the unlucky number. A part of me wants to take it as a sign. Red door, unlucky number, it should set off alarm bells, but I have had enough bad luck in the last year, so I'm not letting a door colour and a number fuel my ridiculous notions.

I watch as Michael unlocks the door and gestures for me to walk in. I do and am struck by the difference in appearance from the stairway to the hallway behind this door. The apartment looks immaculate, and from what I can see has been decorated in clean colours.

The cream carpet beneath my feet compliments the pale-yellow walls. The lounge and kitchen are open-plan, with two separate doors on the right-hand side of the room. I presume one leads to a bedroom and the other a bathroom.

A black, two-seater leather sofa sits underneath a window on the far back wall, and opposite is a large flat screen television, with a coffee table sitting in front of the sofa.

There is a kitchen counter running halfway across the room, separating the lounge space from the kitchen space. A small table and chairs are situated in the middle of the kitchen space, with a fridge freezer just behind it.

I realise that I have taken far too long assessing Michael's apartment, and when my eyes meet his, I find him watching me.

"It's not much, but it suits me," Michael says, seeming to need to explain himself.

"It's lovely," I reply, feeling bad that he obviously thinks that I am not bowled over by where he lives.

"It's not lovely, Lucy, but it does me."

"Michael, there isn't anything wrong with it," I say, gesturing around the room.

"I don't intend on being here forever. It's just a stop gap whilst I save some money for a deposit to buy my own place." I sense a bit of discomfort from him, and I desperately don't want our evening to start on a sour note.

"You said something about cooking?" I ask, changing the subject.

"I did," he replies, giving me a look of relief. "Spaghetti Bolognese okay?"

"Sounds good."

"Would you like a glass of wine before I create my special Bolognese?"

"Yes to the wine. And… special Bolognese?"

"Yeah, it's a secret recipe," he says with a wink. He has a twinkle in his eye, and I like how the conversation is coming easier now that the focus is off of where he lives.

"Are you not going to share the secret with me?" I say in more of a flirty manner.

Michael takes a few steps towards me and leans down, his lips hovering just in front of mine. I feel the air whoosh from my lungs. With him this close, it's hard to focus on anything other than his lips.

"If I told you, then I would have to kill you." His words make me freeze, and my breath hitches.

"What?" I whisper, feeling uneasy. He chuckles, and whatever the glint that I saw in his eyes was just now has gone. The warmth that I'm used to seeing from him has returned.

"Relax, Lucy, I'm just messing around."

"Oh," I say on an exhale.

I am not quite sure how to act, but I am quickly thrown off guard again as Michael's lips brush against mine. I haven't kissed anyone since Tom, so my body instantly tenses from the intimate contact. Michael seems to pick up on my hesitation as he pulls back slightly, breaking the contact between us.

"Sorry," he says. "I didn't mean to overstep the mark."

He is searching my eyes for an answer, and I look at his handsome features.

As I study his chiselled jawline and his full lips, I have two choices. I can either end what is happening between us here and now, or I can let go and move forward with my life.

It doesn't take me long to reach a decision as I press my lips back against Michael's.

I can't keep living in the past.

I can't keep living in fear of being hurt again.

I can't expect every man to be the same as Tom.

Chapter Six

THE MORNING AFTER

I wake up the next morning with a smile on my face. My evening with Michael was wonderful. I may still have my insecurities, but I am determined to beat them.

When I kissed Michael back, after my wobble, it was magical. The way in which he was gentle with me made me like him all the more.

The way that he carried me to his bedroom and made me feel like I was the only person that mattered was incredible.

I am currently laying in Michael's bed, with his arms wrapped around me, and I allow myself to snuggle closer to him as I relive the things that he did to me last night…

Michael picked me up, his lips connected with mine as he carried me to his bedroom.

Gently laying me down, his mouth travelled down my throat, his teeth lightly grazing

my sensitive flesh. He stopped briefly, looking at me for acknowledgement to carry on

as his hand settled on the top of my thigh. All it took was a nod of my head for him to

continue.

Blocking everything out of my mind, I simply let myself enjoy every sensation

running through me.

As I was stripped of my clothes, butterflies went crazy inside of me. Nerves built up, but they were soon put at ease by the feel of Michael's lips, soft as a feather, teasing the inside of my leg. A low groan escaped past my lips as he found my clit with his tongue. It had been a while since I had had any sort of sexual contact with a man, so it didn't take me long to reach my orgasm.

Michael expertly worked me through my release before beginning a slow, gentle rhythm, with himself buried inside of me. I gripped onto his shoulders, my fingers digging into his skin. Our frantic breathing was the only sound in the room. The slow thrusts of his cock making me build to another release.

My body started to tremble, my cries getting louder from the overwhelming pleasure.

When Michael came a few strokes later, I felt like my world had shifted. Shifted in a good way. It was the perfect way for me to be introduced back into the world of 'boy meets girl'. Although dubious at first, I realised that Michael had been the perfect choice of partner for me.

Attentive, sensitive to my needs, and oh-so-ready to make me start forgetting about Tom.

The warm, fuzzy feeling surged through me upon reflection. I am so glad that Michael asked me out, and I am so glad that Kim urged me to follow through and go for that first drink with him. I haven't felt this content in a long time.

Michael stirs, and his arms tighten around me. I smile against his chest, loving the closeness between us.

"Good morning," he says, his voice sounding a little groggy from only just waking up, but no less sexy.

"Morning."

I place a light kiss on his chest, and I allow my lips to travel up to his neck. A deep growl comes from him as I am released from his arms and turned so that I am flat on my back, pinned to the bed by his fine form. He grinds his hips into me, and I open my legs as my pussy cries out for him to be closer.

He brings his head down and starts to gently bite on my bottom lip, and a giggle bubbles out of me. I try to move but he still has me pinned to the bed, not that I am going to complain, of course, but I would like to be able to touch him.

His tongue delves into my mouth, and I arch my back, trying to gain more contact with him.

"Someone's eager this morning," he says, his voice deep and laced with innuendo.

I feel the blush creep across my cheeks from his words. I don't want him to think that I am going to become needy now that we have slept together. I don't want him to be worried about me turning into some kind of bunny-boiler.

"I'm sorry."

"Sorry? Why are you apologising?" He pulls his head back to look at me, and I can see slight concern in his eyes.

"I… um…" *Oh god, he's going to think I'm such an idiot. I don't know what to say. I can't tell him that I am worried that he might think that I am too keen, that would just make me look even worse than I probably look right now.*

I have been out of the dating loop for so long that I have no idea how to act. I don't want him to think badly of me.

"Lucy…" He whispers my name before placing a light kiss on my lips. "You don't need to be nervous around me, and for the record, I'm eager too." His soft smile eases my racing mind. "I like you, and I'm not going anywhere." His gaze turns serious, making my heart pump wildly. "We may not have been going out together for long, but I want this to work. I can see myself falling for you, Lucy, and I really hope that you feel the same way. I don't ever want you to feel like you have to behave a different way around me. Just be yourself, because that is the person that I have grown fond of."

His words stun me, but instead of worrying about how to answer him, I lift my head up and connect my lips with his.

I think that I may have just died and gone to heaven.

His words were what I needed to hear, striking a chord deep within me.

Michael is going to be the one to bring me back to life.

And as our kiss becomes hungrier, I literally do feel like the luckiest woman in the world.

Chapter Seven

LOVE IS BLIND

It has been three months since I first went on a date with Michael, and I can honestly say that it has been the best three months of my life. Even better than when I first started dating Tom.

Michael has been a perfect gentleman in every way. He makes me feel wanted, and I truly hadn't realised how much I had missed that feeling. I have stayed at his every weekend for the last two months. I look forward to Friday nights, knowing that I get to be wrapped up in a bubble with him until Monday morning.

"So, I guess that you will be staying with Michael again tonight?" Kim asks me as we both get our travel coffee mugs ready to take with us to work.

"You guess right." Nothing can wipe the smile off of my face or dampen the fire in my belly.

"Luce, are you sure that you're not rushing things?" Kim asks tentatively. I turn to face her and can see that her brows are knitted together in concern.

"What do you mean? You're the one that pushed for me to go out with him in the first place."

"I know, I just… I don't want you getting hurt again," she says as she bites her bottom lip.

I know that she is genuinely looking out for me, but this is a bit of a turnaround to her previous behaviour as far as my love life is concerned.

"Kim, there's nothing to worry about. I'm having a great time, and I haven't felt this good in forever."

"That's great, but maybe you need to tread carefully where Michael is concerned?"

"What?" I say, turning my head to look at her, my happy feeling suddenly fading. It turns out that the smile can be wiped off of my face, and Kim is the one to achieve it.

"I've heard some things," she tells me.

I can tell that she really doesn't want to be having this conversation with me, but out of respect for our friendship, I decide to hear her out. I won't let myself jump to conclusions until I have heard what she has to say.

"Go on," I urge.

"Oh god, I don't even know if what I have heard is just office gossip or if it's the truth."

"Spit it out, Kim." I can see that she is conflicted. "Just tell me," I say as my heart starts to pump a million miles a minute.

"Well, Nancy on floor five used to go out with him, and she said that he was… That he became—"

"Oh for goodness sake, just say it," I interrupt, losing some patience at her inability to form the words that she needs to.

"Possessive. He was a bit full-on."

"Right… by doing what exactly?"

"She didn't go into detail, she just thought that I should try and warn you."

I already know what Kim is referring to. Nancy and Michael dated for two months, but it fizzled out quickly. They were out one evening and Nancy had gone to the toilet. When a few minutes had passed, Michael wondered where she had got to. He headed for the toilets and found Nancy outside with her tongue down someone else's throat.

"I'm really not that worried about what Nancy has to say." I feel a little relief filter through me at Kim's revelation. I already knew, and that shows that I can trust Michael. He's been open and honest with me, giving me no reason to disbelieve him.

"Are you serious? Do you not want to know what happened?" Kim asks, gobsmacked by my reaction.

"I don't need to know because Michael already told me what went on between them."

"Oh." Kim was not expecting that answer. "And what was his explanation?"

I give Kim a quick recount of what Michael told me, and I can see that she is shocked by Nancy's behaviour.

"But she seems so... vanilla," Kim exclaims.

"Yeah, well, she's clearly not as vanilla as we thought."

"So, it's just a case of a bitter ex then?"

"Exactly."

Chapter Eight

MOVING FORWARD

I don't mention Nancy to Michael when I get to his later on that evening. I don't need to, and I certainly don't want to ruin the mood by bringing her name up.

We're currently laying together on the sofa, Michael with his arms wrapped around me as I snuggle into his chest. Michael let me choose a film to put on, so I decided on a film showcasing female empowerment. It's one of my favourites and Michael has never seen it. The story is brilliant, showing how a woman can have her world rocked in the cruellest way, only for her to come through her heartache and fight to the bitter end.

We're halfway through the film when I feel Michael's lips brush against my ear. I feign ignorance as I continue to watch the film, but my body responds instantly. My nipples pucker and my skin tingles. His tongue traces along my jawline and his arms squeeze me closer to him.

"Do you mind? I'm trying to watch the film," I say teasingly.

Michael chuckles, and the sound makes my insides melt. The fact that I can make him laugh brings me so much pleasure.

He doesn't respond with an answer, instead he plants his lips on mine. I let out a muffled squeal of delight as our tongues dance together, and I forget about the film as we make-out like a couple of horny teenagers.

I don't know how much time passes before Michael breaks our kiss and places his forehead against mine. At some point we manoeuvred our bodies so that I am laying on my back with Michael laying on top of me. My eyes are closed as I enjoy the feel of him encasing me.

"Open your eyes," he whispers, his voice carrying an urgency even though he speaks quietly. I do as he asks and am met with his penetrating gaze.

"Everything okay?" I ask, not being able to decipher the way in which he is looking at me.

"Yeah, everything's fine. More than fine." He takes a deep breath, and his next words literally blow my mind. "I love you."

What?

Did I hear him correctly?

Did he just say that he loves me?

"Sorry, what did you say?" I ask, needing to hear him say it again before I say anything else.

"I said, I love you."

I clamp my mouth shut and blink rapidly. Never in a million years would I have thought that Michael would say those words to me tonight.

"I'm sorry if I have said that to you too soon, but I can't hide how I feel anymore. I don't want to scare you off but—"

I cut him off by placing my fingers over his lips. He abruptly stops speaking and his eyes widen slightly.

This wonderful man has just declared his love for me, and now he is apologising because he is worried about scaring me.

He has done nothing but think about my needs in the last three months, and he has taken everything at a pace that I am comfortable with.

I already know how I feel about him, and I don't want to waste any more time in keeping it to myself.

"I love you too."

Chapter Nine

A BRIGHT BEGINNING

"Miss Fields, we have been reviewing the work that you have done since starting as a temp for us," my boss, Mr Collinson, says as I sit there wondering why I have been called into his office. I can't recall doing anything wrong.

"Your work has been excellent, and you have acquired several new customers for us in a short amount of time. I would like to take this opportunity to offer you a permanent position within the company," he tells me, with a smile on his face.

"Oh, wow!" Now *that* I was not expecting.

"Of course, if you choose to accept the position then it would mean a salary increase for you, and we would like to promote you to marketing manager."

Holy shit! A promotion? Manager?

"You would remain on the floor that you have been working on, and essentially you will be in charge of four other staff members within the marketing team. That team will consist of Beverly Watson, Tony Smith, Henry Walker, and Tyler Morris."

I already know who is on the marketing team, but I am not about to interrupt him. I listen as he discusses my rate of pay and what would be expected of me by taking a management position. With every word that he speaks, I feel my confidence rise.

Mr Collinson doesn't seem to have a bad word to say about my work, and that makes me feel fantastic. I have worked my butt off whilst I have been here, but I never did it to gain a promotion. I did it to keep myself busy. I did it to occupy my mind when Tom and I broke up, and for it to result in this seems like some kind of reward for all of the shit that I have been through.

"That being said," Mr Collinson continues, and I realise that I zoned out for a few minutes there. "You have forty-eight hours in which to make your decision."

"Oh, I don't need to think about it. I accept," I reply, not wanting to waste any time.

"Are you sure, Miss Fields?"

"Absolutely."

This is my fresh start.

New job, loving boyfriend, and a whole new me.

Chapter Ten

SUBTLE DIFFERENCES

"Wow! That's fantastic," Kim says as I fill her in on my conversation with Mr Collinson.

"I can't believe it. I mean, I never expected a promotion." I'm still in a state of shock.

"You deserve it." Kim embraces me in a hug.

"What's going on over here?" I hear Michael say as I break away from Kim and turn to face him with a great big grin plastered on my face.

"Lucy has just been offered a promotion," Kim says excitedly before I can tell him.

"Kim," I scold her gently.

"Sorry, I'm just so excited for you."

I can't be mad at her. She's my closest friend and only wants the best for me.

"Seriously? A promotion?" Michael says, his eyebrows raised in surprise.

"Yeah. Mr Collinson said that he was pleased with my work and that he wanted me to become the marketing manager of this department." My voice is high-pitched with excitement as I speak. "I get to run my own team *and* I get a pay increase."

"Isn't it great?" Kim says to Michael.

"Uh, yeah," he says, no excitement to his tone whatsoever. Kim's smile fades, as does mine.

"What's wrong?" I ask him, wondering why he appears to be unhappy with this turn of events.

"Nothing's wrong. I'm happy for you."

"You don't seem like it," Kim says, and I whirl around to face her.

"Kim, that's enough."

"I'm sorry, Luce, but he should be ecstatic for you," she replies, not bothering to keep her voice down at all. "This is an amazing opportunity, and he has no right to make you feel shit about it."

"He's not making me feel shit," I argue.

"Oh really? So why have you gone from elated to downcast since he came over here?"

"Kimberly—"

"I'm gonna leave you two to it," Michael says, interrupting us.

"Michael, please don't listen to her," I say, needing him to know that I don't agree with what Kim is saying.

"I'll speak to you later," he says before turning his back and walking to his desk.

I feel a sense of dread fill me as I watch his retreating form. Instead of focusing on his reaction, I turn to Kim, my blood boiling at how she behaved.

"What the fuck was that?" I say, not bothering to hide the irritation in my voice.

"What? He was behaving like an arse," she says as she rolls her eyes and folds her arms across her chest, becoming defensive.

"You didn't even give him a chance to speak." I keep my voice as low as I possibly can, seeing as I don't want the whole office to hear us.

"He didn't seem like he wanted to say anything to congratulate you."

"What the hell is the matter with you?" I ask her, outraged that she could have upset Michael for no good reason. "For all you know, he might have had a shitty day, or maybe he didn't want to cause a fuss in the office, or maybe, just maybe, he might have wanted me to be the one to tell him about my promotion but instead he heard it from *you*, because *you* couldn't keep your mouth shut."

I take a second, my breathing a little heavy as I pause my rant at Kim. She has the decency to look a little sheepish in response.

"I don't know what your issue with Michael is," I continue. "And to be quite honest, Kim, I don't really care right now. You were fine about him until you spoke to fucking Nancy, and now all of a sudden my word isn't good enough." I'm mad. Fucking raging, in fact.

"Luce, I didn't mean to——"

"Save it," I say as I hold my hands up in response to her. "I'm going for a walk. The least you can do is cover for me if Mr Collinson comes in here and asks where I am."

I take my jacket off of the back of the chair and turn on my heel, marching for the exit, keeping my head down as I do.

Chapter Eleven

THE START OF THE BREAKDOWN

I'm sat in the park, which is a five-minute walk from the office. I have been gone for half an hour, trying to calm myself down, but I don't feel any better.

I watch as kids run around, screaming and laughing without a care in the world. Parents are sat on the benches, chatting amongst themselves, enjoying the adult conversation. I close my eyes and wish that I could rewind the last hour. Kim had no right to act the way she did. I know that she is just looking out for me, but she hasn't even taken the time to get to know Michael. If she did, then maybe she would see that he is a sweet, caring guy. I'm still not bothered by what Nancy has said, what bothers me is that it is affecting Kim's view of things.

"Hey," I hear Michael's voice say.

I open my eyes and turn my head to look at him. He has a soft smile on his face and his hands are in his trouser pockets. He looks so handsome, but even that can't distract me from the anger that I am feeling.

"Mind if I sit?" he asks, nodding to the empty bench beside me.

"Sure."

He sits down and takes my hands in both of his. "I didn't mean to sound disappointed by your job offer."

"You have nothing to apologise for. Kim is the one who should be apologising."

"She's your friend and she expected me to react differently," he says, sounding so bloody reasonable about her behaviour.

"That's no excuse."

I'm not having him sticking up for her. She was totally out of order.

"I guess I was just a little shocked that she was the one that told me," he admits.

"I didn't want her to. She blurted it out before I had a chance to."

"I know."

"I wanted to tell you tonight, over dinner."

"Dinner?" he asks, his eyebrows raised in question.

"Yeah. I was going to suggest going out after work, but she ruined it."

"She's just excited for you."

"I know that," I say with a sigh. "But it was still inappropriate."

"Does she have a problem with me?" he asks, and I immediately tense up. He sees the change in my body language before I can hide it. "She does."

"It's not you," I say, sounding like a fucking cliché. I was hoping to keep this from him, but I may as well be honest now. "It's Nancy."

"Nancy?" His eyebrows knit together, and I know that what I am about to say is going to annoy him. Hell, it would annoy me if it were the other way around.

"Kim and Nancy were talking the other day and Nancy told her a load of bullshit."

"Like what?" I grimace at his question. "It's okay, Luce, you can tell me." I love that he uses my nickname now. It makes me feel like this is familiar, comfortable, and for keeps.

"Nancy told Kim that things didn't work out between the two of you because you started to become possessive." His eyes widen, but I continue to speak before he can say anything. "I told Kim it was all rubbish, and that Nancy was the one who ruined things between the both of you, but she clearly still has reservations."

"Do you believe what Nancy says?"

"Of course not," I reply instantly.

"Well, then that's all that really matters," he says with a shrug of his shoulders.

"You mean, you're not mad?"

"Mad? No, I'm not mad. I'm a little disappointed that your friend doesn't trust my intentions towards you, but I'm not mad." I lean towards him and place a light kiss on his lips, my love ratcheting up a notch for him. "What was that for?"

"Because you really are amazing," I tell him, meaning it more than ever.

There would have been a time when I was too embarrassed to say this to him, or to any man, but Michael is changing me, and he is changing me for the better.

"So are you, and you're going to be an amazing marketing manager," he says with a smile across his face.

"Thank you."

"Now all I have to do is win Kim's acceptance."

"You don't have to do that."

"I know I don't have to—I want to." And that right there is why this guy is the one that I am supposed to be with. "I just want you to be happy."

"I am," I say. No doubts. No objections. No questions whirling around in my mind.

Michael is putting me back together, one day at a time.

Chapter Twelve

MEDIATION

"Be nice," I say to Kim as we make our way to the restaurant to meet Michael.

"I will be," Kim replies as she tries to be convincing.

Tonight, Kim, Jeremy and I are having dinner with Michael. It was all Michael's idea as he wants to get to know Kim better. It has been two days since Kim and I had our argument, and we have rectified that as much as we can. This is the final step to putting whatever bullshit Nancy has fed her to bed.

"Good. You too, Jeremy," I say as he trails behind both of us.

"Hey, I have no beef with this guy," Jeremy says.

"No, but you are loyal as hell to Kim, and what she says goes," I say.

Jeremy is like a puppy dog when it comes to Kim, so if Kim doesn't like someone, then Jeremy usually follows suit. Kim has the decency to remain quiet as she knows that what I am saying is true. Jeremy, however, appears keen to dispel my theory.

"I do have my own mind, you know? I am capable of choosing whether I like someone or not." I turn around to look at him and even he doesn't look entirely convinced by his words.

"Just be cool."

"I will. Jeez, anyone has got to be better than Tom."

"Jeremy," Kim hisses at him.

"What?" Jeremy says.

"That is so inappropriate," Kim says, hissing her words at him.

"Actually," I interrupt, before they can have one of their regular bickering sessions. "Jeremy's right. Tom was a dick."

I face forward, my head held high, and stride ahead of them both to enter the restaurant where we are meeting Michael. I know that both of them will be shocked by my words as they witnessed how heartbroken I was to find out that Tom wasn't my soulmate, but I've seen the light and have gained perspective in the last few months. In fact, I feel a little bit stupid for spending so long licking my wounds. Tom wasn't meant to be my happy ever after, but Michael is certainly looking like he sure as hell is.

My eyes scan the restaurant in search of Michael, but instead they find the person that the three of us were just talking about.

"Lucy," Tom says, looking shocked to see me.

"Tom," I say with a slight nod of my head. I have no interest in speaking with him, all I want to do is find Michael and make sure that my friends see the type of man that I have fallen in love with.

Tom's mouth has dropped open a little, and I notice how thin his lips are. I never noticed it before. His red hair is longer than when I last saw him and is almost reaching his shoulders. He's also lost weight. Less pudgy, but far from toned, more sinewy.

Good grief, I spent months pining for this guy, and he doesn't hold a candle to Michael.

"Kim, Jeremy," Tom says, acknowledging my friends behind me. I hear Kim murmur something, and Jeremy grunts in response. Tom turns his attention back to me.

"How are you?" he asks in a pitiful tone.

"I'm great thanks, Tom," I reply, a genuine smile on my face.

He is clearly shocked at my response if his wide eyes and dropped jaw are anything to go by. I don't ask how he is because I honestly don't care, and I don't want to drag this conversation out any longer than is necessary.

"You're looking good," he says as he rakes his eyes up and down me. I fidget slightly as I feel uncomfortable. I chose to wear a little black halter-neck dress that is cut to just above the knee. Teamed with my black heels and lace cardigan, I thought that I looked pretty good, but Tom is making me feel icky.

"Thanks," I say awkwardly.

"So—"

"Hey," Michael says as he comes from behind Tom and places a kiss on my cheek, interrupting whatever Tom was about to say.

"Hey," I answer, smiling up at him.

"Wow, you look amazing," Michael says as his eyes drink in my attire. His words elicit an altogether different reaction from me than Tom's did. I feel sexy when Michael says it, not dirty and cheap.

Michael turns his head to register Tom stood in front of me. "Who's this?" he asks me.

"Michael, this is Tom." I don't need to expand on who Tom is, Michael knows all about him.

"Oh." Michael's easy manner is replaced by tension as he turns his full body towards Tom, placing me behind him. It's like he is protecting me, and I would expect nothing less from him.

"Hi," Tom says as he holds his hand out to Michael. I can see the two of them sizing each other up, but Michael has no need to. He's firmly in my heart, and firmly packing way more appeal than Tom.

"Hello," Michael says, but he makes no attempt to shake Tom's out-stretched hand.

"Uh, shall we go and sit at our table?" Kim chimes in from behind me, and I have never been so glad of her interrupting something.

"Yes, let's go," I say as I place my hand in Michael's. My touch seems to bring Michael back to reality as he turns to look at me and smiles. Tom's eyes drop to mine and Michael's hands, and he looks momentarily stunned.

"Oh, are you two…" Tom's voice trails off, almost as if he wasn't supposed to say that out loud.

"Not that it is any of your business, but yes, I am with Michael now," I say, feeling more confident than ever before.

"Oh, right." Tom runs one of his hands through his hair, a move that I used to think was cute but now evokes no reaction in me whatsoever.

"Um, well, you're a lucky guy," Tom says to Michael.

"Yes, I am," Michael retorts. "And you're the daft prick that let her go." I hear Kim struggle to contain her laughter behind me. "But then again, if you hadn't been a daft prick, I may never have had the chance to be with her, so maybe I should be thanking you for not being able to keep your dick in your pants."

I suck in a sharp breath, and Tom looks like he has been sucker-punched. Kim lets out a giggle, and Michael swiftly leads us in the direction of our table.

We step around Tom, and I don't even feel the urge to turn back around to look at him. He has no impact on my life or my feelings anymore.

Michael doesn't stop until we are at the back of the restaurant and at our table. He pulls out my chair and I sit down, replaying what he said to Tom in my head.

Is it ridiculous that Michael's words make me feel special, empowered, and like I am the centre of his world? Because if it is, then so be it. The warmth fluttering through me has me feeling just a little bit smug. Not something I am used to feeling, but I'll take it after how shitty Tom made me feel.

However, my smug feeling lasts for another three seconds before Michael places his lips beside my ear and whispers, "I don't like it when you flirt with other men, Lucy."

"What?" I say as I quickly turn my head to look at him.

His hand comes to the side of my face, blocking us from Kim and Jeremy's view as he whispers, "You, flirting with Tom, I don't like it."

I let out quiet laughter before realising that Michael is totally serious.

"I wasn't flirting with him, Michael. I wouldn't do that. Not now, not ever," I reply adamantly.

"He's your ex, and I don't like you talking to him," Michael says, his eyes burning into mine.

"Oh my god, Michael, I'm so sorry," I say quickly and quietly, realising how awkward it must have been for him having to meet my ex, especially without any warning. Guilt smashes into me with a force that I never thought possible. The last thing I want is for Michael to feel insecure. I know how that feels, and it can destroy you.

"I promise that I wasn't flirting, and I promise that Tom means nothing to me," I say before I place a kiss on his cheek. His hand moves to the nape of my neck and holds me in position, so that his head is now completely blocking me from Kim and Jeremy.

"He better not, Lucy, because I don't think I could handle the thought of losing you," he says before placing his lips on mine, claiming me, showing me how much I mean to him.

I have never in my life experienced the intensity of how Michael feels for me, and it wraps around me like a security blanket; one that I so desperately need.

I'm not worthless, and Michael is showing me that now. It might be a little over the top for some, but when you've had months of feeling vulnerable, you will take love and hold onto it, savour it, be consumed by it.

"Put her down," I hear Kim say before a giggle escapes her.

Michael pulls his lips from mine, gives me a wink, and releases his hold on me before sitting beside me and placing his hand on my knee.

Kim and Jeremy are sat opposite us, and Kim immediately comes to life.

"Oh my god, did you see Tom's face?" Kim asks me as she continues to laugh. "Talk about a deer caught in the headlights."

"I'm sorry about that," Michael says, ever the charming gentleman. "I didn't mean to be so blunt, and I hope that it doesn't affect your opinion of me."

"Affect it? Hell, you have just gone way up in my books, pal," Kim says.

"Hear, hear," Jeremy says as we all burst into laughter.

Michael speaking to Tom like that has broken the ice, and I have a feeling that the rest of the night will unthaw anymore cold feelings towards him.

Chapter Thirteen

A BEAUTIFUL BROMANCE

"Where have the guys gone again?" Kim asks me as we both relax in her lounge, a glass of wine in hand.

"You really don't take any notice of Jeremy when he tells you stuff, do you?" I reply playfully.

"I do for the important stuff, like when he's taking me to dinner, or when he's going to shag me into a state of oblivion," Kim replies, and I spit out the mouthful of wine that I had just taken.

"Oh my god," I say, holding my belly as it starts to hurt from laughing so much.

"Say it like it is," she replies, smiling mischievously.

"I don't think anyone could accuse you of sugar-coating your words."

"I wouldn't want them to either," she replies matter-of-factly. When I have wiped away my tears and regained my breath, I finally answer her question.

"They were going to watch the dog racing and then go for a few drinks afterwards."

"Oh, yes, Jeremy mentioned some racing thing," she says with a wave of her hand.

"In fact, they should be back any moment now," I announce as the front door opens and we hear the laughter of the two men.

Jeremy comes into view first, his sky-blue eyes glazed over, indicating that he has had a little too much to drink, not to mention his blue shirt is no longer tucked in and his floppy blond hair is all in disarray.

"Hey, girls," he slurs as he stumbles over to Kim and leans down to give her a kiss. Unfortunately, he loses his balance and ploughs straight into Kim, knocking her wine all over her.

"Jeremy," she screeches as she struggles to get him off of her.

"Oh shit, sorry, babe, didn't meant to."

"For fuck's sake, man, how old are you?"

"Old enough to know better, yada yada, I know the drill, but we had fun, so I couldn't give a toss right now."

I laugh at their banter, and then my eyes lock with Michael's. He doesn't look anywhere near as drunk as Jeremy, and there is definitely no mistaking the heat in his gaze.

"Hey," I say, putting my wine glass down and standing up.

I walk over to him and snake my arms around his waist. He leans down and places a kiss on my lips, allowing me to taste an essence of whisky on them. I am not a fan of whisky, but on his lips it's not so bad.

"Are you ready to go?" he asks me, and I sense that there is an urgency to get me out of here.

"Oh, sure. Let me just go and get my coat," I say as I move past him and out into the hallway.

Kim is still shrieking at Jeremy to get off of her and I feel a little sorry for him for the hangover that he is going to wake up with tomorrow morning. I put my coat on and make my way back to the lounge.

Michael has taken the liberty of picking up my handbag and is waiting for me to say my goodbyes.

"Kim, I'll give you a call tomorrow," I say as she just sticks her hand in the air to say bye. She is definitely going to have fun trying to get Jeremy to bed, as he seems to be half-asleep already.

I take Michael's hand in mine and lead him out of the house

and out into the fresh air. It's a little chilly and a shiver runs through me.

"Come here," Michael says as he nestles me into his side, so that we can walk back to his place. His arm comforts me and makes me feel safe.

"Did you have fun tonight?" I ask him.

"Yeah, it was okay." He doesn't sound very convincing.

"Well, Jeremy certainly seemed to have enjoyed himself."

"Oh, he definitely did. Now there is a man who can't handle his drink."

"Hmm. He's going to feel so bad in the morning, especially once Kim has dealt with him." I chuckle at the image that conjures in my mind. I have seen Jeremy come back in a state before, and I have witnessed the morning after. Kim will spend the morning playing loud music and singing at the top of her lungs whilst Jeremy whimpers for her to have more sympathy. Kim will tell him that he should know his limits and that it serves him right. Jeremy will then spend the rest of the day creeping around Kim before she finally gives in and they snuggle up and watch a film together.

"I like Jeremy, but I still think that Kim is unsure about me."

"Nonsense. Kim does like you. You proved what I meant to you when you stood up to Tom at the restaurant." I feel his body tense against mine and I know that it is because I mentioned Tom's name. He feels uncomfortable when I mention him, but unfortunately, I can't erase my past, and Tom is a part of that.

"Speaking of which, Tom was at the dog racing tonight."

"Oh, really?" Shit, I hope that doesn't mean that Michael spoke to him.

"Yeah. He came over and chatted to Jeremy for a bit."

"Well, Jeremy thinks that Tom is a wanker, so there's no chance of that becoming a regular thing."

"Hmm." We walk in silence for a few minutes until Michael speaks again. "They seemed to be quite friendly."

"Probably because Jeremy was drunk."

Jeremy is one of those guys that doesn't have a bad bone in his body when he is drunk. He will talk to anyone and is generally just up for a laugh.

"I don't like it, Luce. I don't like Tom being able to reach your friends. The guy is an arsehole, and he hurt you." His tone is dangerous as he speaks, but I just put this down to him not liking my ex.

"There's no need to worry, Tom is irrelevant to my life."

"I still don't like it." His grip on me tightens more, his fingers digging into my skin a little too much, but I don't say anything, I'm more concerned with knocking this insecurity out of him. I stop walking and turn to face him. I place my hands on either side of his face and stare straight into his eyes.

"I am not interested in Tom," I start, saying each word slowly. "The only man that I care about is stood right in front of me. I don't care if Jeremy chats to him because there is nothing that Tom can say that will affect me. He's part of my past, but you are my future."

"Do you mean that?"

"Of course I do."

"I don't ever want you to leave me," he says with a new-found urgency in his tone.

"I'm not going to leave you."

"Promise?"

"I promise."

"You're mine and no one else's."

"Yes, Michael, I'm yours."

Chapter Fourteen

COMMITMENT

"Move in with me," Michael says as we lay in bed together, our limbs entwined. I shoot up to a sitting position and swivel my body around so that I can look at him.

"What?" I whisper, astounded.

"Move in with me." It's not a question, more of a statement.

"Are you serious?" I ask. We have only been together for five months, so it seems a little rushed.

"I have never been more serious about anything before." He sits up and cups my face in his hands. "I love you, and I want to wake up to you every morning. I don't want to be apart from you."

"But we haven't been together for that long... what happens if it doesn't work out?" My insecurities rear their head. I moved in with Tom and it all went to shit. I don't want that to happen with Michael.

"Why wouldn't it work out?"

"I don't know. Life throws unexpected shit at you," I say with a shrug of my shoulders.

"It does, but I think that we're stronger together. Aren't you sick of staying at Kim's? Don't you want to have a place that you can call your own?"

"Well, yeah, eventually——"

"Then why not now?" He looks so hopeful, and I don't want my worries to wipe the hope off of his face.

"I just… what we have is great, and I love being with you… I don't want anything to change."

"It won't change. It will be better. Don't you want to try it?"

"You've given this a lot of thought, haven't you?" I ask him, seeing it written across his face.

"I've thought about it since the moment that I realised I was in love with you." His words blow me away. I've never met a man as deep as him. "So what do you say? Give it a chance? A trial run, if that makes it seem less scary?"

I love him.

He loves me.

We're happy.

Living together is the next step.

A trial run. I can do that. I can take it one day at a time.

"Okay, let's do it."

Chapter Fifteen

THE HONEYMOON PERIOD

A week has passed since I moved in with Michael, and if every week continues to be like this past one, then moving in here was the best decision that I ever made.

We go to work together, we come home together, we cook together, we pretty much do everything together, and I love it. Of course this is the honeymoon period, so I am not expecting it to be like this forever, but I am enjoying every moment of it while it lasts.

"Babe, I've run the bath," Michael shouts from the bathroom.

We got in from work tonight and Michael could see that I had had a stressful day filled with client meetings, so he ordered me to sit on the sofa whilst he cooked dinner. I did as I was told, and he made a delicious meal of spaghetti carbonara before he cleaned up and then announced that he was running me a relaxing bath.

I smile as I make my way to the bathroom to be greeted by the subtle scent of lavender bubble bath hitting my nostrils. I open the bathroom door and am treated to the view of Michael already being sat in the bathtub, with candles placed along the windowsill.

My jaw drops open slightly at his romantic gesture.

"Oh, Michael."

"What? Too much?" he teases. He knows that I am a sucker for a bit of romance.

"No, I've just never been treated like this before." I feel my eyes well up from the emotions that I am experiencing, and all because of a fucking bath.

"Hey," he says soothingly. "I didn't do it to make you cry."

"Oh, I know that," I say, trying to shake off my overreaction. "I'm just being silly. It's been a long day, so just ignore me."

"Never." I smile at him and thank my lucky stars that he came into my life. "Are you going to shut that door and get in here, or am I going to have to drag you in?"

I laugh at his playful nature. He's been more relaxed since I moved in here. He doesn't worry about me as much, and I guess that is because he knows where I am and that I'm okay.

I start to undress, and he watches my every move. I make it more seductive than it should be to take your clothes off for a bath, but it makes Michael look at me like he wants to devour me on the spot, so I make an exception.

Once I am undressed, I take the couple of steps to the bathtub and get in. I squeal when Michael suddenly grabs me and pulls me to him.

"Michael," I say, laughing.

"You were taking too long."

He presses his lips against mine and my whole world comes to a stop. It always does when he touches me. It's as if nothing else exists.

His hands stroke up and down my arms, leaving a trail of goose-bumps. When he pulls back from me, he smiles and signals for me to turn around, so that I am leant against him. I comply and enjoy the warmth of the water and the warmth of his body. I close my eyes, lean my head back, and feel Michael nibbling on my ear a few seconds later. I groan in pleasure.

"You know that I love you more than anything, right?" he whispers in my ear.

"More than anything?" I tease. I already know that he does, but I like to have fun with him. He nods, but his face doesn't look playful, he looks serious.

"I never want you to doubt my love for you."

"Okay."

"I will always be here for you."

"Michael, what's wrong?" I know there is something troubling him. I can see it in his eyes.

"There is nothing wrong, I just wanted you to know," he replies, trying to be casual but failing miserably. I bring one of my hands up to his face and place it on his cheek.

"Please talk to me."

I hear him sigh as he struggles with whether to tell me or not. I wait patiently as he battles with his inner turmoil.

"I don't like you working with Tyler."

"What?" I ask with a little humour in my voice. That is definitely not what I was expecting to hear from him.

"It's not funny, Luce. I don't like him, and I don't like him around you."

"Why not? What's he done?" I turn my body so that I can gauge Michael's reaction. His jaw is set firm and his whole body radiates tension. I guess he doesn't find it easy to tell me how he is feeling sometimes.

"He fancies you."

I burst out laughing at his statement. "Tyler?"

"Yeah. Don't fucking laugh at me, Lucy. I didn't tell you so that you would make fun of me." His tone grows quiet but assertive and makes me stop laughing immediately.

"I'm sorry," I say, feeling a little guilty that I reacted in that way.

"I should think so." He looks pissed off, and I want to rescue what was turning out to be a relaxing evening.

"Michael, I don't know why you think that Tyler fancies me, but even if he did, it wouldn't make any difference. I don't fancy him. He's a young kid who likes to flaunt the fact that he enjoys a bit of banter. He does it with everybody." It really is as simple as that.

"I don't like it," he repeats, jaw clenched.

"Well, I can have a word with him and tell him to tone it down, how about that?" I suggest, hoping to end this matter sharpish.

"I just can't bear the thought of anyone taking you away from me, and if anyone tried, then I don't know what I would do."

"I told you that I'm not going anywhere, so stop worrying," I say as I place a light kiss on his lips and return back to my original position of leaning against him.

I can still feel that Michael's body is tense, so I decide to give him a little something to help him relax. My hand skims up his thigh until I can hold his length in my hands. I shuffle forward a bit and wrap my fingers around him. I pump slowly to start with, but as Michael's breathing becomes more rapid, so does my hand. I work him until he releases all of his pent-up tension in the form of an orgasm.

Once finished, I lean back against him and relish in the fact that I can pleasure him. He wraps his arms around the front of me and holds me against him.

"Mine," he whispers, and that simple word elicits so much emotion within me.

He just wants to be with me and look after me, and I'm okay with that.

Chapter Sixteen

SILLY MISTAKES

"You guys are so cute together," Kim says as Michael and Jeremy go to the bar to get us more drinks.

"I know. God, Kim, I'm so damn lucky to have found him."

"Well, he is so much better for you than Tom ever was." She has grown fond of Michael over the last couple of months, which I am incredibly pleased about. It didn't take long for her to dismiss her perception that Michael wasn't right for me. Kim has finally realised that Nancy is just some bitter ex that is intent on trying to ruin what Michael and I have.

"I mean, Tom never celebrated your six-month anniversary, but Michael, he's like the guy that is too good to be true."

"He is," I say as I look at Michael through lust-filled eyes. He's leaning against the bar, his muscular arms on display, his handsome face smiling at something Jeremy is saying.

"I'm glad that you found him," Kim says seriously, placing her hand on my arm to gain my attention.

"Thank you."

"I just wish that I had never listened to Nancy."

"It's all water under the bridge. We all know the truth, and that's all that matters."

"Absolutely," Kim says as she picks up her wine glass and drains the last mouthful.

"Hi, ladies," a voice says, making both of us turn our heads in its direction.

"Oh, Tyler," I say, caught off guard at his appearance.

"Hey, Tyler," Kim says.

"Are you two on your own?" Tyler asks us. I am about to answer but Kim beats me to it.

"Well, we are for now," Kim says with a wink.

"Oh cool. Can I join you for a bit?"

"Sure," Kim answers.

I feel a bit of my relaxation fade as Tyler sits next to me. Michael doesn't like Tyler and he won't be happy with Kim inviting him to sit with us. I can kind of see why Michael might have a problem, I mean, Tyler is only nineteen years old, he's young, he's easy on the eye with his black hair styled so that it goes up in a small quiff at the front, his bright green eyes sparkle, and he's got a toned physique, but all I see is a boy. He's not a man, and he's definitely nothing like my Michael.

"So, what are two good-looking ladies like you doing sat on their own?" Tyler says at the most inappropriate moment, as Michael and Jeremy come back to the table. I freeze when I see Michael's jaw clench.

"They're not on their own," Michael bites out behind gritted teeth.

"Oh, hey, man," Tyler says.

"Who's this?" Jeremy asks. His reaction is the polar opposite to Michael's. Jeremy is smiling, whereas Michael looks like he wants to drag Tyler out of here.

"This is Tyler, he works with us," Kim says, before adding, "And Lucy is Tyler's boss."

"Nice to meet you," Jeremy says, extending his hand to Tyler. The two guys shake hands and Michael still hasn't moved. He catches my eye, and I can see a fire blazing in his, and not in a good way. He looks to Tyler, and I can literally see him assessing how close Tyler is sat to me. I need to rectify this situation quickly.

"Excuse me, Tyler, can I just get past you so that I can use the toilet," I say.

"Sure." Tyler jumps up and lets me slide out of the booth.

"Thanks."

I walk away, hoping that Michael calms down by the time that I get back from the toilets. Tyler is just a work colleague, and Michael needs to rein in his dislike of him.

I enter the toilets, use the facilities, and wash up after. Taking a few deep breaths, I exit the toilets and am stunned as I am abruptly pulled into a small hallway, just by the side of the toilets. I let out a yelp from the fingers that are gripped tightly around my arm. I am about to scream when I am turned around and I come face to face with Michael.

"Shit, Michael, you scared the hell out of me." I breathe a sigh of relief that it is just him. I go to move my arm away, but his grip is still tight, and I wince from the pain.

"Michael, you're hurting me," I say, realising that he probably doesn't register his own strength. I expect him to loosen up, but he doesn't. He just stares at me, a dark look in his eyes.

"Michael, please," I say, trying to keep myself calm.

"I told you that I didn't like Tyler."

"Michael, can you just let go of my arm?" The pain is intensifying, and I am pretty sure that his grip has tightened even more.

"You told me that he meant nothing to you. Did you lie?"

"What?"

"Did you lie about how you feel about him?"

"No, of course not," I reply, flabbergasted at his reaction.

"Then why the fuck is he sat by you?"

"Because Kim told him that he could sit with us."

"Don't blame Kim. He was sat by *you*."

"So?" I fail to see where he is going with this.

"So? Is that all you have to say?" His tone is firm, not wavering one little bit.

"What do you want me to say?" Panic starts to rise within me. I've never seen Michael this angry before. I don't know how to deal with it.

"I want you to tell me that you're not a liar, Lucy. I want you to realise how much I fucking love you, and how much another man sitting next to you pisses me off."

"I haven't lied," I answer quietly.

"Are you sure about that?"

"Yes, Michael, for fuck's sake. Kim said he could sit down, and he just sat. That's it, there is nothing more to it than that. You guys came back over thirty seconds later. Now, will you please let go of my arm?" I can see the emotional war that he is battling on the inside, and it breaks my heart. "I love you, Michael, nothing is going to change that."

I watch as his face softens, and he seems to finally register his hand gripping my arm.

"Shit," he says as he lets me go. I let out a little cry of relief as my arm drops to my side, a dull throb pulsing through it. "Oh my god, I'm so sorry, Lucy. I just… you being around other guys makes me crazy. I didn't mean to hurt you. I would never——"

"Shhh," I say as I place a finger over his lips. "I know."

I can feel Michael trembling as I push my body against his and wrap my arms around his waist. His arms envelope me fiercely. He whispers that he is sorry over and over again.

I know that he didn't mean it.

He loves me, and love can make us do silly things.

Chapter Seventeen

WORK WOES

I have now been in my current management job for three months. Things have been going well, until today. Today has been awful, and I have no idea how I am going to make the situation better.

It was all going well, until Mr Collinson announced that I had to work with Tyler on a certain project. Michael overheard, and my world has currently dimmed a little.

Tyler is ecstatic that he gets to work on this new idea. I smiled and told him that it would be a great opportunity, all the while wondering how I was going to get out of it. I went and spoke to Mr Collinson, but he wouldn't hear of me handing the project to anyone else, and Tyler shows the most promise on my team, so the decision is final.

Michael didn't wait for me to walk home with him. Not a good sign.

I say goodbye to Kim and make my way out of the building. Once I step foot outside, my brave face slips and I let the inner turmoil overtake me. Each step towards my home with Michael fills me with dread. This is just going to fuel Michael's insecurities. We got over the scenario in the pub the other day, but this is going to be ten times worse.

I walk as slowly as I can, but I reach the floor of our flat far too quickly. With a heavy heart, I make my way up to door thirteen.

Putting my key in the lock, I turn it and open the door slightly. There is no sound.

Maybe he hasn't come home yet? Maybe he has gone for a drink to clear his head?

I walk in, shutting the door behind me. I plod along the hallway and into the open-plan kitchen and lounge area, and I jump a mile when I notice Michael sat on the sofa, staring at a blank television screen.

"Shit, you made me jump," I say, following it with a nervous laugh.

He doesn't turn to look at me, doesn't even acknowledge me walking into the room.

I place my bag on the kitchen table and take off my jacket, hooking it over one of the chairs. I slip my shoes off and softly pad my way across to him.

Stopping in front of him, I lower myself down until I am kneeling before him. Placing my hands on his knees, I know that I need to put his fears to rest.

Michael doesn't believe that he deserves me, but he couldn't be farther from the truth.

He still stares ahead, almost as if he is looking through me. It hurts, but I know that inside he is hurting more than me. It might seem a little dramatic to some, but Michael loves hard, and I suppose I understand his fear of me leaving. Hell, I've lived through a break-up that almost destroyed me, so I have every sympathy for Michael.

"Michael, I know that today hasn't been great, but I tried everything that I could to get out of working on this project. Mr Collinson wouldn't let me give it to someone else. At this point, I can't see that there is any more that I can do to change his mind." I speak softly, needing him to understand how much I tried. I notice his jaw ticking in response and I carry on speaking. "I don't want this to cause problems between us. Tyler is just a work colleague; he means nothing to me. I would never do anything to jeopardise what we have together." I sound like I am pleading, but it's actually just reassurance for Michael.

"Anything?" he says, his eyes finally focusing on me.

"Yes."

"Quit."

"Pardon?" I don't think that I heard him correctly.

"I said, quit. Quit your job."

I kneel there for a few moments, my mouth opening and closing like a fish.

Quit my job?

Give up on something that I am genuinely starting to enjoy?

"I can't do that, Michael."

"Why not? You said that you would do anything."

"Yes, I know, but I'm not giving up on my career. I enjoy my job." His eyes narrow on me, and I feel a coldness sweep through my body.

"And do you enjoy it because you get to be the big boss lady? Or do you enjoy it because you secretly love the attention that Tyler gives you?" His voice is low and dark.

"Michael, what are you talking about?" I am so confused right now. This is going in a direction that I never saw coming.

"Don't tell me that you don't enjoy a young guy giving you puppy-dog-eyes all day long, I see the way he looks at you, and the way you look at him. Your eyes sparkle, and they don't do that with me anymore."

"What? This is crazy, of course I don't look at him in any specific way. What the hell is the matter with you, Michael?" My patience is wearing thin.

There are only so many times that I can tell him that I only want him. There are only so many ways in which I can word it so that maybe, just maybe, one of those words gets through to him.

I stand up, folding my arms across my chest. Michael looks up at me, unrelenting with his hard stare.

"What's the matter with me?" He rises to his feet until he is looking down at me instead of up. "What's the matter with me?" he repeats. "You really want to fucking know?" His voice gets louder and louder with each word until he is shouting in my face.

"Michael, please, calm down," I say as I place my hands on his chest. He looks at my hands, and then, without warning, he smacks them away. I start to tremble, panic rising as I enter an unknown element to our relationship.

"I will not fucking calm down, and you will tell me why the hell you are fucking with me," he shouts, rage evident in his whole demeanour. "Am I just some kind of plaything for you to keep on a string? Am I just here until the next best thing comes along? AM I JUST SOME STAND-IN UNTIL YOU FIND SOMEONE ELSE?"

"No!" I shout back at him, terrified by his reaction.

"Do I mean that little to you that you would use me like this?"

I take a step back from him, and he steps forwards. "Michael, you're scaring me," I whisper.

"Oh, really?" He smirks. "And you don't think that you scare me?" My head is spinning from all of the things that he is saying. None of it makes sense. "It scares me how much I feel for you, Lucy, do you ever think about that?"

I don't answer as I am not sure what I am supposed to say, but that is a mistake. He grabs both of my arms and shakes me backwards and forwards. I start to cry, tears falling rapidly down my cheeks. I ask him to stop, but it just seems to make him angrier.

"I love you and all you seem to do is throw it back in my face." He stops shaking me abruptly, and my legs give out. I drop to the floor, my back hitting the coffee table. I pull my legs up to me, wrapping my arms around them to bring me some comfort. My body is shaking uncontrollably, and I feel like my world has completely shifted.

The Michael that I love doesn't appear to be inside the man stood in front of me. The man in front of me is like a stranger.

Michael leans down until he is level with my face. I shy away from him, but he grips my chin with his thumb and forefinger and moves my head so that I am looking straight at him.

"I will not be taken for a fool, Lucy." He lets go of me and stands back up, walking away from me.

A few seconds later, I hear the flat door open and then slam shut again. I let out a loud cry of relief at his swift exit. I sit on the floor for an age, unable to comprehend everything that just happened.

I have no words.

I didn't know that Michael, and I don't wish to ever meet him again.

Chapter Eighteen

SORRY

I am still sat on the floor of the lounge when I hear the front door open and close. I'm cold and I feel numb, confused, and scared. I don't move as I hear footsteps make their way into the kitchen. I keep my head down, my arms still wrapped around my legs. The footsteps continue until they are stood next to me, and I close my eyes, waiting to see what is going to happen. I don't want to say or do anything to make this situation worse. I feel Michael kneel down beside me, the smell of alcohol wafting towards me. My body starts to shake again, and the air becomes tense.

"Baby," he says, soft and more like the Michael that I love. I still don't turn to him though. I can't bring myself to look at him right now.

"Lucy, I'm so sorry." Those words bring a fresh wave of tears. I let them fall silently as I hold my breath.

"Please will you look at me." I shake my head from side to side. I can't. I hear him take in a deep breath and blow it back out.

"I didn't mean any of it, I was being an idiot and I let myself get carried away. I would never intentionally hurt you... I love you; you are my life. I just get so scared that you're going to leave me, and I hate the thought of it."

At this point, I hear him sniff, and it makes me look at him. I watch as tears fall down his cheeks. I can see the remorse on his face. He's embarrassed by his actions.

"Please don't hate me." His control goes, leaving in its place a man that sobs, a man that needs a little reassurance and help to regain his composure. As much as it shouldn't, my heart goes out to him.

I move for the first time in hours and turn to him, placing my arms around him as we both let out the grief that we are feeling. His arms lock around my waist, and mine lock around his shoulders.

"I'm so fucking sorry," he says between sobs. I let my fingers run through his hair as I pull my face back and place a kiss on his lips.

"It's only you that I want," I whisper.

Michael nuzzles his head in the crook of my neck, and I feel his tears on my skin. "I didn't mean to frighten you."

"I know."

"I love you."

"I know."

"I'm sorry."

Chapter Nineteen

FORGIVENESS

I wake up in bed to see that the time is half past ten in the morning.

"Shit," I say as I sit bolt upright. I'm ridiculously late for work. I scramble out of the bed and dash over to the wardrobe, grabbing some work clothes and frantically trying to think of an excuse as to why I'm late. I take out a smart trouser-suit and grab some lingerie from the chest of drawers, but I come to a stop when the bedroom door opens to reveal Michael stood there with a mug in each hand.

"Hey," he says as he comes over and gives me a kiss on the cheek.

"Why didn't you wake me sooner?" I ask him, but before I give him chance to respond, I ask another question. "Why aren't you at work as well?"

"Calm down," he says as he walks over to the bedside table and places the mugs down. "I called into work this morning and told them that we wouldn't be in today."

"What? Why?"

"Because I figured that we both needed the rest."

"I can't have a sick day, Michael, I have too much work to do."

"I figured that, so I called Kim an hour ago and she's going to drop your work laptop round on her lunch break." He comes over to me and takes the clothes out of my hands, placing them on the end of the bed.

"I think it would be good for it to be just us today," he says as he takes my hands in his and rubs his thumbs over my knuckles. "I want to make up for last night."

"There's no need," I reply, a soft smile forming on my face.

"Yes, there is. I acted like a complete jerk, and I need to make it up to you."

"Honestly, I'm fine."

"I feel bad, and I want to do something to show that I'm sorry."

"You have already apologised more than once."

"Please, Lucy." His eyes are pleading with me, and I decide to give in. If he wants to make it up to me, then who am I to stop him?

"Well, seeing as you have got work covered, how about you start by showing me just how sorry you are by taking me to bed?" I waggle my eyebrows and step back, undoing the top button on my pyjamas. The smile that graces his face is wicked, and the sparkle that I love so much makes an appearance in his eyes. He prowls towards me, and I keep moving back until I am pressed up against the wall. His chest collides with mine and my heartbeat speeds up a notch.

"Now *that* I can do." He grabs me and turns me, pushing me onto the bed. I squeal with delight and take pleasure in the fact that playful Michael has returned.

As he kisses my neck and runs his hands up and down my body, I let the feeling of the moment overtake my senses.

He's sorry and I love him.

He knows that he was wrong, and I guess I just need to be more careful of how I interact with Tyler.

Michael is my life now, and I will do anything that I can to help him see that.

Chapter Twenty

REALITY CHECK

I have been spoilt for the last week. Michael has bought me flowers, chocolates, and a beautiful silver necklace. I have told him that he doesn't need to, but he chooses to ignore that, insisting that I should only have the best in life.

I am currently sat with Kim, grabbing a bite to eat on our lunch break. We chose to go to a café located in the centre of town, so that it will give us a chance to catch up without office ears listening in.

"So, how's things with you and Michael?" Kim asks me whilst nibbling on a chip.

"It's good," I reply, with what I imagine is a dreamy look on my face.

"That's great." I can tell that she wants to say something else, so I put down my knife and fork and focus all of my attention on her.

"What's up?" I ask, one eyebrow raised.

"I don't want you to get mad with me."

"Why would I get mad?"

"Because it's about Michael."

"Oh for goodness sake, just say it," I reply, wondering what information she thinks she knows now. I know that she is probably worried that we might have an argument, like we did previously, but it's better that she says whatever is on her mind.

I fold my arms across my chest and lean back in the chair, waiting for her to speak. She wipes her hands on a napkin and leans her elbows on the table.

"Tyler came to speak to me yesterday."

"Okay."

"He said that Michael had pulled him to one side and had a word with him." At this news, my interest piques. Michael hasn't said anything about speaking to Tyler, but I know that Kim wouldn't lie to me.

"Go on," I urge her.

"Tyler said that Michael firmly warned him off of you. He said that Michael was a little intimidating and he found it weird that Michael was warning him off of you when you're just work colleagues."

I roll my eyes and unfold my arms, my hands going to my head to rub my temples as I feel a headache coming on.

"Oh, jeez."

"Has Michael got a problem with Tyler?" Kim asks.

"Yeah, I guess you could say that."

"Why?" I really don't want to answer Kim's question, but I have to. She needs to see why Michael would act this way. I don't want her to think badly of him.

"Michael seems to think that Tyler has a bit of a thing for me. I've told him that he is being ridiculous, but I guess that he still harbours a little insecurity about the issue."

"The whole office knows that Tyler fancies you," Kim says, as if it's no big deal.

"What?" I screech a little too loudly.

"He's a young lad with a crush on his boss. How did you not know this?" Kim asks me, looking a little surprised that I haven't noticed anything.

"Because I didn't. I just thought that Michael was being a little paranoid."

"Well, he is, and he isn't. He's being paranoid because Tyler is young and good-looking."

"Is he?" I ask, screwing my nose up a little. I don't know why I even bother to ask this question because I know that Tyler is good-looking.

"Oh yeah," Kim confirms with a chuckle. "But as for him being paranoid of you and Tyler hooking up, he needs to get over that shit, and quick. It's plainly obvious to anyone with eyes that you love the bones of him."

"Wait, really?"

"Christ's sake, Lucy, you bat your eyes at him all day long. Your body language changes when you are near him, and far be it for me to say this, but you look like you need to take a cold shower when you speak to him." I feel my cheeks get warm, and I imagine that I am the colour of a beetroot. "It's okay to be like that, you know. You're in love, it's cute, but just get Michael under control. He doesn't need to go around warning off every guy that fancies you."

I don't relish the idea of continuing this conversation, so I simply give Kim the answer that she is looking for.

"Sure. I'll speak to him about it tonight."

Chapter Twenty-One

CONFRONTATION

"Hey, babe, you ready to get out of here and spend the weekend in bed?" Michael asks me, a big grin on his face.

"Ugh, you two are so bleurgh," Kim says from her desk, making both Michael and I laugh.

"It's only because you're jealous," I tease her. She pokes her tongue out at me, making me laugh harder.

"Of course I am. Whilst you two are still in some sort of lust-filled haze, I get to spend the weekend listening to Jeremy shout at the football scores whilst farting intermittently."

"Oh, Kim, stop," I say as I hold my stomach, which is starting to ache from all of the laughing.

"Seriously, it's going to be the highlight of my weekend."

"Maybe we could all get together Saturday night?" I suggest, seeing as we haven't all been out together for a while.

"That sounds awesome! It's a definite date, so no calling me to cancel because you're too busy fucking each other's brains out," Kim says, and I blow her a kiss whilst grabbing my stuff to get the hell out of here.

Michael places his arm around my shoulders and we walk out of the office and make the short journey home.

Once we get through the front door, I head straight to the kitchen and click the kettle on to make a cup of tea.

"Would you like a drink?" I shout so that Michael can hear me in the hallway.

"No, I'm good," he answers from behind me. I take a mug out of the cupboard and pick up the television remote, flicking it on so that I can see what films are on this evening.

"What do you fancy watching tonight?" I ask Michael as he stands in the doorway to the kitchen.

"I don't mind," he says with a shrug of his shoulders.

"You know that if you don't say now then you will be subjected to two hours of a pure unfiltered chick flick, don't you?" I say teasingly.

"Why did you say that we would go out tomorrow night?" he says, abruptly changing the subject. The kettle clicks to signal that it has boiled, and I busy myself making my drink.

"I just thought that it might be nice. We always have fun when we hang out with Kim and Jeremy, and I couldn't stand the thought of Kim's weekend consisting of farting, belching, and shouting out the football scores," I say with a chuckle. I stir my drink and put the kettle back on its stand. "Why, is there a problem?"

"It would have been nice to have been consulted beforehand."

"Oh, sorry, I didn't think that you would mind." He nods his head at me and makes a grumbling noise. "If it's a problem then we can take a rain check?"

"Yeah, right, and have Kim storming round here to drag us out anyway?"

"Did we have plans to do something?" I ask, racking my brains in case I have forgotten anything.

"Not exactly."

"Well then, there's no problem," I say with a smile as I pick up my drink and place it on the kitchen table.

"You don't ever see anything as a problem," he mutters quietly.

"And what is that supposed to mean?" I ask, placing my hand on my hip defiantly. He scoffs and throws his hands into the air in exasperation.

"Oh, come on, Lucy, we always do what you want to do. When do you ever ask me what I want to do?"

"Are you being serious right now?"

"Totally." I'm taken aback at his attitude.

I cast my mind back and try to think of a time when I have asked him what he wants to do. Unfortunately, I can't think of one, but that is because he always tells me that it's my choice and that he only wants to be doing what I want to do.

I feel anger bubble up within me at the way in which he speaks to me sometimes, and as much as I have tried to hide my frustration over the whole Tyler issue, I can no longer bite my tongue.

"And I suppose that speaking to Tyler behind my back shows consideration on your part, does it?" My tone comes out harsher than I expect it to, but at this point, I'm just pissed off with the way he's acting.

"Did Tyler tell you that?"

"It doesn't matter who told me, it matters that you did it."

"Why? Because you don't want to upset lover-boy?" Michael's tone is sarcastic, and I don't care for it one little bit.

"Oh for fuck's sake, Michael, how many times do I have to tell you that I don't see Tyler in that way?" I shout, frustration rolling off of me in waves.

"Liar."

"I'm not fucking lying."

"You swore to me. You promised me." He moves towards me, but this time I don't step back. I stay routed to the spot, prepared to fight this one out just to make him see how ridiculous he is being. "You said that you loved me, that you didn't want to hurt me." Another step, a clenched jaw.

"And I meant it!"

"Then why the fuck do you continue to flirt with him? It's embarrassing." Another step.

"I do no such thing."

"People have started noticing. People have started talking. You think that I don't hear them saying that our relationship must be on its last legs if you're flirting with Tyler? You think I don't see the looks that they give me; pitying and sorrowful? I don't like being looked at in that way."

"Seriously, Michael, you are way off of the mark."

"Am I? AM I?" he shouts in my face, coming to a stop in front of me.

"YES!" I shout back, feeling good that I am standing up for myself.

"Did you just shout at me?" he says, his tone quiet, his eyes glaring.

"I sure did." He will not make me feel bad, I have done nothing wrong. I lift my head up high. I will not back down.

"So now you have grown a backbone?"

"I've always had a backbone; I just choose not to use it unless I have to."

"Well, shall I show you what happens when you defy me?"

"Go on then," I goad him, the anger burning through me.

I have no idea what is going on in that mind of his, but I don't have long before I find out. A few tense seconds tick by, and then, from out of nowhere, his hand comes across my face, slapping me hard.

My head snaps to the side from the force of it, and from the fact that I was unprepared for something like that to happen. My hand flies up to my cheek as it starts to sting. Tears well in my eyes from the pain.

I look back to Michael, expecting to see remorse, but he still just looks mad. Beyond mad. Fucking furious, in fact.

He moves his face towards mine and I bite my bottom lip to stop it from trembling.

"If you didn't act like such a fucking flirt, then I wouldn't have had to do that," he sneers.

He hit me.

He fucking hit me.

Oh my god, breathe.

Calm down.

It's going to be okay.

He didn't mean to.

It was an accident, surely?

"I don't think that I need to explain my actions here. I think that it is perfectly clear why I had to react like that," Michael says before he turns his back on me and walks to the kitchen doorway. Before disappearing from view, he turns back around to face me. "But just so we're clear, you made me do this. You took my love for granted and pushed me to do this. Maybe next time you will think twice before you disrespect me, Lucy." I don't miss the evil tone that his voice has taken on.

With that, he walks down the hallway and into the bedroom. I let out a whoosh of air as I fight to contain the tears that emerge.

Maybe next time?

Next time?

There won't be a fucking next time.

Chapter Twenty-Two

TRAPPED

I'm fucked.

Completely and utterly fucked.

I sit on Kim's sofa, nursing my bruised cheek. I left the apartment last night as soon as Michael shut the bedroom door. It only took seconds for me to grab my bag and go. I didn't want to waste any time by staying there a moment longer than I needed to. God knows what else he would have done with the mood that he was in.

He has tried calling my phone all day and all night long. He's left voicemails, text messages, and every single one states how sorry he is. And my pathetically-in-love heart is melting towards him.

I'm sorry.

I love you.

It won't happen again.

I'm an idiot.

I lost control.

I've never done anything like it before.

I love you.

I love you.

I fucking love you.

His words play on repeat in my head, and I am hopeless to stop them. The problem right now is that Michael has made me happier than I ever have been. I see him as my soulmate. He's my one and only, and how the hell am I supposed to turn away from that feeling?

"Are you not going to tell me what happened?" Kim asks as she comes into the lounge and flops down beside me.

"I told you, it was just a stupid argument."

"Must have been pretty bad for you to come here," she replies softly.

"Well, I just needed some time to cool off."

"You did, or he did?"

"Me. Michael hasn't done anything wrong."

Liar, liar, pants on fire.

"So, what was it about?" I didn't say much to Kim last night because I was in such a state when I turned up here. She just hugged me, and I must have eventually fallen asleep on the sofa as I woke up to find that I had been covered in a blanket.

"Tyler." I don't need to lie on that front. Most of it was about Tyler.

"Oh."

"Yeah."

"So you confronted him?" she asks.

"Yep."

"And?"

"To be honest, I don't really want to talk about it. I said some things that I shouldn't have said, and I felt that I needed to leave Michael in peace."

"It can't have been that bad, Luce?"

"Oh, it was."

"Well, you were in quite a state. How's your face?" she asks me.

"It aches a little, but it will be fine. It's my own stupid fault."

"Hardly surprising that you tripped and fell, considering you could barely stand up straight when I saw you."

"Yeah, I kind of overreacted a little." I smile sheepishly and pray to God that she buys my lame-ass excuse. She doesn't have time to respond as the doorbell rings and she stands up to go and answer it.

I lay my head down on the cushion of the sofa, but I am soon sitting up straight when I hear Michael's voice. I don't know how to act as I hear Kim invite him inside.

Fuck. What the hell am I meant to do now?

With my mind racing, Michael walks into the lounge, and he looks terrible. Red-rimmed eyes, slight stubble, and nothing but regret in his eyes.

"Hey," he greets me quietly.

"Hey."

"I'll just give you guys a moment," Kim says before I hear her go up the stairs to give us some privacy.

"I, um, I didn't know if I should come and find you or not," he mutters, clearly stuck for words.

"Well, you did and here I am."

"Lucy, I didn't mean to—"

"To what? Hit me?" I only say the words loud enough so that Michael can hear me. I don't need Kim catching wind of this as she would flip her lid.

He nods and hangs his head in shame. "I don't know what came over me. I've been going out of my mind with worry since last night."

"Oh really? Is that just because you're worried about who I have told?"

His head springs up and he looks genuinely upset that I have said this. "Of course not. Tell whoever you like, just please come back home with me." I laugh at his reference to the word 'home'.

"Aren't you supposed to be safe in your own home?"

"You are safe."

"Yeah, away from you." I can't even muster up the energy to be nice to him. I shouldn't have to anyway, I'm not the one in the wrong here.

"Please don't say that. I love you."

"So you said."

"You don't believe me?" He looks gobsmacked, but I don't really know what else he was expecting from me.

"It's pretty hard to when I have a pain in my cheek that reminds me otherwise." I point to my face and turn my head so that he can see that my cheek is a light purple colour. His face pales at the sight, and I can see that even he is shocked by how it looks.

"I honestly didn't mean it. I just get scared about losing you. God dammit, Lucy, you make me crazy. Crazy about you, crazy for you, crazy about everything to do with you. I promise that I won't ever do anything like this again." I stay silent. I need time. I need to process all of this. I can't decide what to do on a whim. "I feel lost without you with me."

"That's not my fault."

"I know, it's mine. I'm the one with the jealousy issue, but I swear, I will get help if you want me to. I will do anything, just so long as you come back to me." His begging chips away at a little of the icy exterior that I have on display. My heart is screaming at me to go to him, forgive him, let him prove his love. Yet my head is telling me to remain cautious, to keep my guard up and protect myself.

"I just need to be away from you right now," I say without looking at him. If I look at him then I will want to go back with him, and I can't give in this easily. I need to show him that he can't treat me this way.

"Okay," he says quietly. "But you're coming back to me, right?"

The silence stretches between us for a few minutes.

Am I?

Can I?

Should I?

Would he hit me again?

Is he a monster underneath the caring man that I have grown to love?

I let my eyes meet his and give him the only answer that I can.

"I don't know."

Even as the words come out of my mouth, I know that I will return to him when I am ready.

I love him, and everyone deserves a second chance, right?

Chapter Twenty-Three

FAMILIAR FACES

"Don't you wanna dance?" Kim asks me as she sways to the beat of the music.

"Not really," I reply. I have no energy to dance, and I still feel conflicted over what happened with Michael last night.

"I hate seeing you like this."

"Well, I did tell you that I would be no fun tonight."

Kim persuaded me to come out with her tonight and forget about the disagreement that I have had with Michael.

Yeah, as if it is that easy.

Obviously, Kim still doesn't know the whole truth, so I can't really blame her for not realising what a shitty situation I am in. "If you want to go and dance then I will be fine here by myself," I tell her.

"I'm not leaving you alone."

"Kim, I will be fine," I reassure her. "I'm not going to break."

"Okay, but I will be keeping an eye on you," she says as she points to me. I smile at her and watch as she sashays her way onto the dance floor.

I try to switch my mind off, but it's no good, everything is still so raw. I place my hand on my cheek and wince as it still hurts to touch. I managed to cover up the faint bruise with make-up, so that no one would notice it whilst I was out.

I want to cry.

I want to hide.

I want to rewind and go back forty-eight hours.

I don't want to be a woman in this kind of predicament.

"Well, well, if it isn't Lucy Fields," I hear a voice say from behind me. I whirl around on my seat and am stunned by the person that is stood there.

"Oh my god... Cal?" I say, the sight of him momentarily taking my breath away. He nods at me, and I find myself standing off of my seat and throwing my arms around him.

"Hey," he says softly as he wraps his arms around my waist and hugs me back. His familiarity is my undoing. I haven't seen him in so long and it has shattered the last of my resolve. I let a few tears leak from my eyes as I tighten my hold on him.

Before Michael, the last place that I truly felt whole was with Cal. He was my first love, my first everything in an emotional sense. We always had a strong bond, and although I pushed aside any romantic feelings that I used to hold for him, our bond will always be special.

"What's going on, Luce?" he asks me, and I loosen my hold on him, feeling incredibly stupid for letting my guard down. I step back and swipe underneath my eyes.

"Oh, nothing, it's just a nice surprise seeing you is all." I smile but Cal doesn't buy it.

"Lucy, I have known you for a long time, and I know when you're lying to me."

"I'm not lying," I try to insist, but he's always been the one person that I can't fool.

Cal stands there and assesses me for a few seconds. I can see that he doesn't believe me, and I hate that I am having to lie, but I can't tell him about Michael. I haven't seen or spoken to Cal since he left to go travelling eighteen months ago. Sure, he sent me postcards intermittently, to let me know that he was okay, but I haven't received one since I left Tom. For all I know, he could still have been sending them, but Tom wouldn't think to pass them on to me. He's too selfish to think of anyone other than himself. In fact, Cal doesn't even know that I have split up with Tom.

"Okay, seeing as I haven't seen you for so long, I will let it slide, *for now*. How about I go and get us both a drink and then we can reacquaint ourselves?" he says, and I nod in response. He goes to walk away but turns back to ask me another question. "I'm guessing Kim is here somewhere, and I'm guessing that she will want a drink too?"

"You guess right," I reply, loving how easily we flow together. It's always been the same.

"Be as quick as I can." He walks over to the bar, and I sit back down on the stool.

Well, I didn't see that one coming.

I watch as Cal saunters to the bar, looking nothing less than perfection. He's my best guy friend and seeing him again has reinforced how much I have missed him.

Cal and I go way back, as do Cal, Kim and Jeremy. Cal is another County Hill School survivor, and we were the foursome that never broke up. The awesome foursome, as the kids nicknamed us.

From the moment that Cal and I became friends, I knew that he would always hold a special place in my heart. We've been through so much together, and I harboured strong feelings for him for a long time. I never acted on them because his friendship meant too much to me. I would rather be friends with him than be nothing at all.

So, I was the girl that was in love with a guy who didn't have a fucking clue, and I was the girl that had to watch him go through girlfriends, his eyes always passing over me.

It took a long time for me to shove my love for Cal into a box and lock it away, a box never to be opened again. Sure, I allow myself to love him as a friend, and that will never change, but he will always be the one that got away.

It's crazy to see him here now, looking so healthy and full of life, whilst I sit here feeling broken and lifeless on the inside. A feeling that I didn't think I would associate with Michael, but here we are, at the shittiest point in our relationship.

I push thoughts of Michael away and focus solely on Cal, needing the distraction.

Cal Bailey—six-foot-three, arms so big that they are threatening to bust out of his T-shirt, thick thighs, and buns of steel. His body is like a work of art. As he walks back towards me with the drinks, I rake my eyes over his face, and fuck if it doesn't do a little something to me. You would have to be blind not to appreciate the beauty of Cal. Strong jawline, chiselled features, full lips, straight nose, brown hair that is long enough to run your fingers through and leave a little messy, and then he has the most gorgeous royal-blue eyes. Eyes that I haven't seen in so long—eyes that I used to dream about, and ones that have haunted me since I was twelve.

As Cal places the drinks on the table, I realise that I have never been so pleased to see him in my life. Kim may be my best friend, but Cal was always the one that I ran to for advice first. He's always been a rock to me, and when he left to go travelling all those months ago, he took a little piece of me with him.

But now that he is here, I am going to have to put on one hell of an act to cover up my emotions. Cal is going to be harder to hide stuff from than Kim.

It seems that my life just got a little bit more complicated.

Chapter Twenty-Four

PLAYING CATCH UP

"So, how long have you been back?" I ask Cal as I stare at him as if he is some sort of mirage before me.

"I got back two days ago."

"And how was it? Did you travel everywhere that you wanted to?" I am intrigued by his bravery to go it alone and discover new places.

"It was awesome, Luce. The sights, the cultures of different countries. I can't describe it other than to say that it was the most amazing experience of my life. Did you get any of my postcards?" he asks, and I give him a nod to let him know that I have.

He takes a sip of his beer and continues to speak. "I actually called round to your place yesterday, but it turns out that you don't live there anymore."

"Uh… No… No, I don't."

"Hmmm. Tom seemed a little shaken at my appearance, but when he realised that I didn't know that you had moved out, he seemed to relax a little."

"I bet."

Tom was always wary of Cal, hated the bond that we had, knew that Cal would always have my back. I guess Tom felt threatened by Cal, but that's still no excuse for him cheating on me. I never gave him any reason to think that I was going to go off with Cal, and Cal didn't disrespect Tom either. Well, not openly anyway.

"What happened?" Cal asks as he sips his beer.

"Do we have to talk about me? Can't I just listen to stories from your travels?"

"Nuh uh, babe, you're not getting out of telling me that easily. My stories can wait for now." See what I mean? Cal is a hard man to hide from.

"Well, to cut a long story short. Tom cheated on me with Carley —I found them in bed together. I moved out, stayed with Kim, and then I met a guy called Michael who works at the same place as me. I moved in with him not long ago, but let's just say that we are on rocky ground right now." Rocky ground… that is the fucking understatement of the year.

I can see Cal watching me, assessing my body language, and I am scared to death that he is going to see right through me, see the truth that I am desperate to hide.

"Tom slept with Carley?"

"Yep."

"You don't still speak to her, do you?"

"Hell no. She burned her bridges with me the minute that she got into my bed with Tom."

"Your bed?"

"Oh yeah," I say with a scoff. "Talk about being disrespected in the worst way possible."

"Shit, Luce, I'm sorry all of that happened. And I'm sorry that I wasn't here for you." Cal looks distraught that he missed one of the most painful parts of my life, but I don't want him to feel bad. It wasn't his fault, and I know now that it wasn't mine.

"Don't be silly, you have no need to be sorry." I give him a soft smile and his hand covers mine, sending a warmth surging through me. "I missed you."

"I missed you too."

"Ahhhhh! Cal!" I hear Kim shriek as she comes over and wraps her arms around him from behind, making both of us laugh.

"Hey, Kimmie," Cal says.

"Bloody hell, aren't you a sight for sore eyes?" she says, taking in his appearance. "Great tan, muscular arms, still got that cheeky smile and glint in your eye, good haircut, damn, I need to get me some sun."

I laugh harder at her assessment, but my laughter gets cut short as a pain shoots along my cheek. Cal notices my abrupt silence and the slight wince on my face.

"You okay?" he asks, his brow furrowed.

"Oh yeah, I'm fine, I just—"

"Fell over the other night and bashed her cheek," Kim finishes for me.

"Kim, you really need to stop doing that," I scold her.

"Stop doing what?"

"Finishing my sentences for me. It's really annoying."

She gives me a wink and sips her drink, taking a seat opposite me.

"How did you fall?" Cal asks.

"I blame her boyfriend," Kim replies, once again answering for me. I glare at her, and she rolls her eyes, hops off of the bar stool, and gives us a wave as she returns to the dance floor.

"Why would she blame your boyfriend, Lucy?" Cal looks concerned, and this is exactly what I was afraid of. Cal will lose his shit if he ever finds out that Michael hit me, and I don't want to paint Michael in a bad light. He made a mistake, and it would be unfair of me to have Cal judging him before he has met him.

I also don't want Cal getting involved in my relationship. I don't want Michael thinking that Cal and I share anything more than friendship.

"We had an argument, I stormed out and went to Kim's, but on the way to hers I fell and hit my cheek. It's really no big deal, it just hurts a little if I smile too much," I say, trying to make light of the situation, more to myself that anyone else.

"Tell me about this Michael," Cal says, his eyes boring into mine.

Oh fuck. Here we go, Lucy, time to act out the best fucking performance of your life.

Chapter Twenty-Five

GOING BACK

I knock on the door and wait.

The seconds tick by.

The sound of footsteps walking to the door are as clear as day.

The turn of the key.

The opening of the door.

The look on his face.

My heart pumps wildly.

Butterflies flutter in my stomach from nerves and from the sight of him.

He did wrong, I know that.

But I love him.

I can't switch it off.

I need to give him another chance.

I want this to work.

I will not be a victim, and I will make that clear.

I walk forwards, he stands still.

I reach up, kiss his lips, enjoy the taste of him.

"Hi." I break the silence.

He stands there gobsmacked.

I hope he still wants me.

I hope he still loves me.
"You came back." His words are quiet.
"I did."
He scoops me up in his arms.
I smile.
I don't want the smile to fade.
I'm done with being hurt.
I just want to be happy.

Chapter Twenty-Six

ALL IS QUIET

Monday morning has whizzed by, and it is nearly lunchtime. I have spent most of my morning trying to concentrate on work, but I keep thinking about last night.

Michael and I reunited, and it was wonderful.

Michael promised again and again that he would never hurt me, and I believe him. I could see how sorry he was. We made love, and then he held me in his arms all night long. I didn't think that I could love him anymore, but last night made me realise that I can. I love him deeply, and I know that he feels the same about me.

"Can we break for lunch now?" Tyler asks, jolting me out of my thoughts, and I see that the clock says that it is just after one.

"Sure."

"Great, I'm starving. See you in an hour." Tyler grabs his coat from the back of his chair and exits the small project room that we have been holed up in all morning. Our deadline for our project is looming, but I am pleased with the progress we have made. I am hoping to blow our potential new client out of the water with our idea for their product.

I gather some papers together and take them with me to the

main office and back to my desk. I intend to work through lunch, seeing as I have been less productive than usual this morning.

Walking to my desk, my eyes drift across the room to where Michael sits, but he isn't there. He must have gone out to get his lunch from the deli across the street—he loves their home-made slices of pizza.

I sit at my desk and put the papers in front of me and am about to grab my sandwich from my desk drawer when I hear a familiar voice speak.

"Fancy grabbing a bite to eat?" Cal says, a big smile on his face as he stops in front of my desk.

Jesus, he looks good enough to eat. Dark denim jeans, a white T-Shirt with a blue zip-up jacket over it, and that glorious smile of his that has made me feel weak at the knees many times over the course of our friendship. Fuck. Rein it in, Lucy, no need to ogle your *friend*. And God forbid that Michael sees him, I haven't even mentioned that my friend Cal has returned from the road trip of his life. I don't even want to have that conversation with Michael right now, not when we've only just made up.

"What are you doing here?" I ask Cal, trying to cover up how ridiculously flustered I feel.

"Oh nice, make a guy feel welcome, Luce," he answers teasingly.

"Sorry," I reply with a chuckle. "I'm just surprised to see you here."

"Well, I was in town and thought that I would stop by on the off chance that you were free to come to lunch with me." Cal used to stop by all the time before he went away. Kim and I would frequently have lunch with him.

"I was planning on working through lunch."

"Seriously? A guy has been back in the country a few days and his closest friend is going to turn him down so that she can work?" I see the cheeky glint in his eye, and I can't help but dismiss my idea of working.

"When you put it like that, how can I refuse?" When Cal is around, it's safe to say that all fucking reasoning goes out of my head. Michael will be pissed if he finds out, but then again, Cal and I are just friends, so really, he has nothing to worry about. *Yeah, okay, Luce, you keep telling yourself that. It's not like you haven't had feelings for Cal for-fucking-ever.* I shake my head to rid myself of my thoughts. Lock it up in the box. Throw the fucking key away.

"Exactly," Cal says, smiling.

I stand up, putting my jacket on and grabbing my bag from the back of my chair.

"Where's Kim?" he asks.

"She's got the week off," I inform him.

"So I get you all to myself?"

"You sure do."

"Lucky me," he replies, making me smile. I link my arm through his as he escorts me out of the office.

"Usual place?" he says, and I nod at him. We are still so in sync even after all the time that he has been away.

We walk to Harvey's Café and find a table to sit at, by the window. I take my jacket off and hang it on the back of the chair whilst Cal looks over the menu.

"Nothing changes here, does it?" he says as he sees that the menu is exactly the same as when he left.

"Nope."

"It's nice. I like that some things don't change." I don't miss the hidden meaning behind his words. He is referring to the friendship that we share.

"You talking about the food or something else?"

"Both," he replies, confirming what I already knew with a smile.

The waitress comes over and asks if we are ready to order. I opt for a caramel latte and tuna melt sandwich. Cal orders a black coffee and the chicken salad with a bowl of fries, just as I knew that he would. The waitress bounces off, taking our menus with her, and Cal and I engage in some light conversation.

Our food and drinks arrive ten minutes later, and I take a bite of my sandwich, enjoying the sensations that it is eliciting on my taste buds. I haven't been to this place in so long that I forgot just how good the food was.

"So, have you and Michael figured things out?" Cal asks me as he takes a bite of his salad.

"Yes. I went back last night, and everything is fine now."

"Do you want to talk about the argument you two had?"

"Not really." No way in hell do I want to discuss it. It's done, over, finished.

"Okay. When do I get to meet him?"

"Jesus, Cal, you have only just got back. Do you not have anyone else that you want to see before you give my boyfriend the Spanish inquisition?" I say, injecting a little humour into the conversation. I need to tell Michael about Cal before any meeting happens. My heart speeds up at just the mere thought.

"I've seen my family, and I met up with Joe and Fletch last night," he says with a shrug of his shoulders. "Plus, you're my favourite person, so I want to meet the guy that you're keeping house with."

"You can meet him soon."

"How soon?"

"Cal," I say his name in a warning tone.

"What?" He feigns ignorance, but I know that he is just looking out for me. He always has.

"I love that you're back home, but I need to tell Michael about you before I introduce you to him."

"He doesn't know that we're friends?" Cal looks a little put out as he asks this question, and I feel bad that I haven't thought to bring him up in conversation before now.

"Well, I've mentioned your name in passing," I say pathetically.

"He knows that we're friends, right?"

"Sure." My voice is a little too high-pitched as I answer. I can feel his eyes on me as I look down and finish my sandwich, but I avoid his stare.

Michael doesn't know much about Cal because I haven't told him. When I first started dating Michael, I mentioned that I had a friend who was travelling, but I didn't know when he would be coming back home. Then time ran away with me, and Cal didn't get mentioned again.

As I realise this, I see what a shitty thing that is to do. Cal is an important part of my life, and I should have made that clear to Michael, but with Cal gone, I didn't feel the need to explain.

"You are happy, aren't you?" Cal asks me, interrupting my thoughts.

"Yes." I am happy, but that feeling of dread firmly settles in the pit of my stomach at the thought of speaking to Michael. I am just hoping that, now that we are back on track, he takes the news well.

Chapter Twenty-Seven

UNEXPECTED INTRODUCTIONS

"Let me walk you up," Cal offers as we come to a stop outside of the office building that I work in.

"There's no need, honestly."

"I know there is no need, I want to."

"God, were you always this insistent before you went away?" I remark, smiling.

"Not quite as bad but being away makes you re-evaluate life. Makes you appreciate things and people more." His answer is a little more serious than I expected.

"Okay then."

"After you," he says as he opens the door and gestures for me to walk in. I roll my eyes, but I can't help the warm feeling within me.

I climb the stairs, Cal trailing behind me, and when I enter the main office, I immediately flick my eyes to Michael's desk. He's still not there and I breathe a sigh of relief. I walk to my desk and place my bag down before turning back to look at Cal.

"Thanks for lunch, Cal."

"No problem. You can buy the next one," he says with a wink.

"Sure thing."

Cal leans in to give me a hug, and I accept his embrace. I am smiling, but the smile is soon wiped from my face when I see the office door open, revealing that Michael has just walked in. I quickly move back and let my arms flop down to my sides.

"Lucy?" Cal asks me questioningly, clearly wondering why my manner has changed in the space of a few seconds. I don't respond. I just watch as Michael makes his way towards us.

Cal notices my attention is elsewhere and he turns his head to see that Michael has come to a stop behind him. I watch as the two men size each other up, and I inwardly groan. I didn't want Michael to find out about Cal this way. I would hate to walk in and see him hugging some other woman.

"Who's this?" Michael asks, addressing his question to me but keeping his gaze on Cal.

"I'm Cal, and you must be Michael." Cal holds his hand out for Michael to shake, but I can tell that Michael would rather be sticking pins in his eyes than accepting a handshake from a guy that he doesn't know. Begrudgingly, Michael takes Cal's hand, but he lets go as soon as he possibly can.

"And who is Cal exactly?" Michael asks, letting his gaze wander over to me. I gulp down the lump that has appeared in my throat and answer the question, so as not to provoke any suspicion from either man.

"Cal is an old friend who recently returned from travelling."

"I see."

"It's nice to meet you," Cal says.

"I wish that I could say the same, but Lucy has never mentioned you before." I can feel both sets of eyes on me, and I wish that the ground would swallow me up.

"I did, Michael, but it was when we first started dating." I feel hot. Suffocated.

"Well, that was a long time ago."

"How about we all go for drinks on Friday night and then we can get to know each other?" Cal suggests.

I freeze in position, waiting to see what Michael's response will be. A few seconds tick by before he answers. "Okay."

"Great, I'll give you a call, Luce, and we can arrange where to go and what time to meet," Cal says before leaning in and placing a kiss on my cheek. "Speak soon."

Cal says bye to Michael and then walks out of the office, the door closing behind him sounding louder than ever before.

"So, I guess that we have some things to talk about when we get home," Michael says before he walks away and leaves me with an even bigger sense of dread.

Chapter Twenty-Eight

WALKING ON EGGSHELLS

Michael had to practically drag me away from my desk this evening. I didn't want to go home. I had been dreading it all afternoon. Now I am here, sat on the sofa, waiting for the argument to erupt. Michael is pouring us both a glass of wine, and he is taking his sweet time about it. I don't know whether it just seems like he is going slow, or whether he is purposely making me sweat just a little bit more. If it is the latter, then it's working.

Nerves radiate through me.

My legs are jigging up and down, and my fingers are picking at imaginary thread on my skirt.

Michael puts the wine back in the fridge and makes his way over to me. Each step has me wanting to stand up and get the hell out of here. I don't want a confrontation. I don't want a repeat of the other night, and I also don't want him to see just how scared I am of his reaction.

Be strong, Lucy.

He won't hurt you again.

He promised that he wouldn't.

No matter how many times I repeat this to myself, I still jump slightly when Michael sits beside me, passes me my glass, and places his hand on my knee.

"You don't need to be so nervous," he says as he sips his wine and then places the glass on the coffee table. I swig the wine, gulping down as much as I can to settle my nerves.

This isn't normal, Lucy.

No one should be made to feel this way.

I will my mind to shut up.

"Now, let's have that chat, shall we?" he says with a hint of annoyance in his tone.

"I didn't know that Cal was going to turn up, I swear." My words come out rushed. I can't get them out quick enough.

"It's okay, you can't help someone coming to see you at work." I look at him, feeling a little confused. I thought that he would have been more than pissed off by now, but he appears so calm and collected, the complete opposite to me. "Why don't you tell me about how long you have known him, and how you became friends."

Okay. He just wants an explanation. That I can do.

"We met when we were at high school together. Cal, Kim, Jeremy and I were inseparable, and we have been friends ever since. Cal went travelling eighteen months ago, and no one had any idea when he would be back."

"So, why not tell me about him?"

"I did."

"Not really. You may have mentioned his name, but you never said much more."

"I didn't feel there was any need to. He wasn't even in the country. I figured that when he came back, I would just introduce the two of you." I glug back more wine. I just want this conversation to be over.

"And do you want to go out on Friday night as he suggested?" I can't figure out if Michael wants me to say yes or no, so all I can do is try and decipher what he wants to do.

"It would be nice for you guys to get to know one another, but it's not urgent. We don't have to go on Friday if you don't want to…"

"Oh, I think that it is urgent. I mean, it's not every day that I walk in the office and find some other guy giving you a hug."

"I'm sorry," I reply automatically.

"No need. He's your *friend*." He smiles at me, but it isn't genuine. "As long as you guys have never passed the friend zone, then we should all get on just fine."

I laugh nervously. Thank fuck I kept my feelings for Cal hidden away. I couldn't be doing with anyone accidentally letting slip how I used to lust after him all the damn time.

Michael took this news better than expected, and I don't want to say anything to pull his trigger and piss him off, so I just smile sweetly and let him put his arm around me, pulling me to his side.

I know that I am going to be on pins and needles waiting for Friday, and I'm probably going to be a bloody wreck on the day itself, but for now, all I can do is grin and bear it.

Relax, Lucy.

Chill.

Even as I tell myself those words, I don't believe that I know the meaning of relaxed anymore, not when I'm around Michael.

It shouldn't be this way, should it?

Am I overreacting?

Am I the one making too big a deal out of this?

I guess only time will tell.

Chapter Twenty-Nine

WHAT COULD GO WRONG?

I have been on edge all day, and now, as I get ready for tonight, I fight back the urge to cancel the whole thing.

I have chosen to wear my navy-blue jumpsuit, paired with my silver heels. I have made my make-up more dramatic, and I have popped in my silver hoop earrings to match my silver bracelet. I have straightened my hair and left it down, a look I don't often go for as I favour shoving my hair in a ponytail so that it doesn't get in my way. I refuse to think about why I'm making more effort with my appearance than normal. It has absolutely nothing to do with Cal, nothing whatsoever.

Michael has decided to wear his smart black trousers, light blue shirt, and black dress shoes. He looks so handsome—something that I have already told him a couple of times tonight. He didn't say too much about my outfit choice, but I put that down to him feeling a bit out of his depth at spending the evening with Cal.

"You ready to go?" I ask him as he fiddles with his cufflinks.

"Sure."

I grab my cardigan, draping it around my shoulders, and follow Michael out of the apartment as we make our way to Alan's. The air is a little chilly and I shiver as we walk along the road. Michael puts his arm around my shoulders and pulls me to his side.

"Better?" he asks, a softness appearing on his face that I haven't seen much of this week.

"Much," I reply, smiling up at him.

We walk the rest of the way in silence, but it is an easy silence. More like when we first started dating.

"Are Kim and Jeremy coming tonight?" Michael asks me.

"No, they had to go and visit Jeremy's parents, something that Kim has been avoiding for a few months."

"Why?"

"Because Jeremy's parents disapprove of their relationship. They think that Jeremy can do better."

"Oh."

"I feel sorry for Kim having to deal with them."

"Have you met them before?"

"Yeah, a couple of times. They are complete and utter snobs, and if you haven't got a high-powered job or you don't earn a ridiculous salary per year, then they view you as beneath them."

"Why does Kim bother to visit then?"

"She does it for Jeremy, because she loves him, and she knows that he needs her support when he sees them. They don't exactly sing Jeremy's praises either."

"Wow, they sound like arseholes."

I laugh at his answer. "I guess you could call them that, although I have heard Kim call them much worse."

"I bet."

We reach Alan's and Michael opens the door for me, letting me walk ahead of him. The place is busy as people emerge for a night of drinking and dancing the night away after working all week.

I scan the room, looking for Cal, and spot him sitting at a table to the far right, just along from the bar. He sees me immediately and waves me over. I take Michael's hand in mine and lead the way. When we reach Cal, I see that he has already got a bottle of wine on the table and a couple of beers.

"Hey," he says as he leans in and kisses my cheek before greeting Michael with a smile. "I hope you don't mind, but I got some drinks in for us all."

"No, we don't mind," I answer as I sit on one of the chairs, Michael sitting next to me. Cal sits back down and starts to undo the bottle of wine.

"Are you a beer or a wine man, Michael?" Cal asks, completely at ease with this meeting.

"Beer."

Cal hands Michael a bottle of beer and then hands me a glass of wine.

"So, how are you both?" Cal asks, to which I reply good, and Michael mutters the same.

"Any luck in finding a job yet?" I ask Cal, knowing that he mentioned that he was looking the other day.

"There are a few that have caught my eye, but I'm just going to see what happens."

"You're not going back travelling?" Michael asks, and I'm pleased that he feels that he can contribute to the conversation.

"No, not anytime soon anyway."

"But don't you enjoy it?" Michael pushes on.

"Of course, the whole experience is amazing, but you do get homesick after a while, and I'm ready to be stuck in one place rather than roaming several."

"Fair enough," Michael replies, and then chugs back about half of his beer. I place my hand on his knee as a reassuring gesture that he is doing great.

"So, Michael, tell me about yourself," Cal says, and I feel a little tension build up within me. Michael doesn't like being questioned.

"What do you want to know?" Michael responds, placing his hand over mine and squeezing slightly.

"Let's start with how you two met," Cal suggests.

"Didn't you already tell him when you had lunch the other day?" Michael asks me.

"I didn't go into detail, but Cal knows that we both work together."

"Uh huh." Michael turns his attention back to Cal and regales him with a story of how he swept me off of my feet nearly a year ago.

A year? Already? Jesus, time really does fly.

"It was love at first sight for me," Michael says, which gains my attention. I smile, but I feel anything but happy right now. I can see a slight glint in Michael's eye, which tells me that he isn't pleased with how things are going. He doesn't feel comfortable, and having to look like he is… it's making this more frustrating for him.

"So, nearly a year, huh?" Cal says, sipping beer from his bottle.

"Yep," I reply, a little too eagerly.

"What are you going to do to celebrate?" Cal asks.

"It's a surprise," Michael says, before I have chance to.

"A surprise?" I ask, a little shocked that he has something in mind.

"Yeah. You don't think that I would let our one-year anniversary go by without doing something special, do you?" Michael says as he leans closer and places a light kiss on my lips. I shake my head in response.

Wow. He hasn't surprised me for a while. Maybe I am finally getting the old Michael back? The one that doesn't mind meeting my friends, the one that makes me feel loved and safe. Me giving him a second chance seems to be working.

"You look after her," Cal says, breaking mine and Michael's gaze away from one another.

"I intend to," Michael replies, a little too defensively.

"This woman means the world to me, and I won't stand by and let her be hurt again." Time almost stops as Cal speaks his mind. I want to erase what he has said, I don't want it to put Michael in a bad mood.

"I don't plan on hurting her," Michael retorts, and I can see that his jaw is clenched tight.

"Good, then we won't have any problems," Cal says with a forced smile on his face.

I want to ask him what the hell he is doing, but I know full well what this is. This is Cal reasserting himself in my life after being absent for so long. This is Cal making up for not being around when Tom shattered my world. This is Cal being the protective friend that he always has been. But what Cal doesn't know is that his words could provoke Michael. His words could be Michael's undoing, but I pray like fuck that they aren't.

Chapter Thirty

PUNISHMENT

The front door slams shut.

I run for the bedroom.

I don't get too far ahead of Michael though.

As I go to crawl under the duvet, fingers curl around my ankle.

Panic rises.

Nausea takes hold.

Fight or flight.

"Please don't," I plead, my voice a whisper.

There is no reply.

I am dragged from the bed, my bum smacking onto the floor with a thud.

A pain shoots up my back, but I ignore it.

I need to stay alert.

"Michael, please can we just talk about this?"

Still no answer.

The blood is pumping in my ears.

I'm dragged along the floor and out of the bedroom.

I whimper like a dog about to get told off for doing something wrong.

Except... I haven't done anything wrong.

I'm positive I haven't. Have I?

My mind is a jumble of thoughts and questions as I am brought to a halt on the kitchen floor.

The lino feels cool against my skin.

I go to sit up but am pushed back down.

Michael's foot on my face, pushing until my head is flat on the floor.

I think I am going to pass out.

I can't control my racing heart.

His foot leaves my face, and then I see him walk away. He sits on the sofa and just looks at me, a mixture of love and hate in his eyes.

"Please—"

"Shut the fuck up," he snarls at me, and I comply immediately.

He's angry.

I need to go careful.

I believed his promises.

I believed that he wouldn't hurt me again.

Was I wrong to give him another chance?

"You humiliated me tonight."

"I didn't—"

"I told you to shut up, and I expect you to do as I say." His stern look has me clamping my lips together.

When he is sure that I am going to remain silent, he continues to speak. "Cal doesn't seem to like me, and I have no idea why that would be. The only conclusion that I can come to is that you have told him things about me. You have told him lies, because Kim and Jeremy don't have an issue with me, so why the fuck should Cal?"

I stay silent.

He told me to stay silent.

"I guess I have more to teach you, Lucy. I thought that you understood. I thought that we had got past all these mind games."

Mind games? I'm not playing any mind games.

"As your punishment for disrespecting me, you can sleep there tonight." He nods to the kitchen floor. "And you're not to move until I say so."

He's lost his fucking mind.

He's supposed to love me, look after me, protect me.

He stands and comes towards me.

I close my eyes and wait for what he is going to do next.

His footsteps stop next to me, but I keep my eyes down, not daring to look at him to see the rage that I know is there.

"Why do you do this, Lucy? You keep making mistakes."

I hear him sigh, and then his footsteps resume. He walks past me, and a few seconds later, I hear the bedroom door shut.

I need the toilet, but he told me not to move.

I need a blanket, but he told me not to move.

I don't deserve to be treated like this.

I could run, but he would just come after me—of *that*, I am sure.

I didn't do anything wrong, and I'm being punished anyway.

My mind is full of questions, none of which I have the answers to.

The first tear falls.

And then another.

I sob silently.

I can't make any noise as it would only anger Michael more.

So I stay put and take the punishment.

Anything for a quiet life.

Chapter Thirty-One

HE'S GOT ME

"Get up." Michael's stern voice makes me open my eyes.

I groggily push myself up off of the floor, every part of me is aching from the discomfort of laying here all night. I slowly move onto my knees to get to my feet, but it obviously isn't quick enough for Michael as he grabs my arm and pulls me to a standing position. I feel dizzy and it takes a moment for it to pass.

"Sit," is his next instruction. He pulls out one of the chairs at the kitchen table and I sit my weary body down.

I'm shaking where I am so cold, and probably traumatised from being treated so badly. Michael doesn't say another word as he busies himself putting the kettle on and taking two mugs out of the cupboard. I watch him in a daze.

How can he treat me this way?

He's supposed to love me.

It's the same questions that circled on a loop in my mind all night long.

I rub my sore eyes and stifle a yawn. I can't do anything that might trigger a reaction from him. It's only Saturday morning, and I don't want to spend my whole weekend paying for whatever the hell Michael thinks that I did wrong.

"Here," he says as he places a hot mug of coffee in front of me.

"Thank you," I whisper, my throat dry and hoarse. Michael pulls the chair opposite me out and takes a seat.

"Do you want to talk about last night?" I shake my head at him. I have no desire to figure out whatever was going on in his mind. "Okay. Do you understand why I had to act the way that I did?" I'm guessing that this is the part where I am supposed to say yes and behave like the good girlfriend. "I take it that from your silence that you do." It's not a question. More of a statement. "I don't like having to get like that. I don't enjoy it." I look up at him with disbelief.

He doesn't enjoy it? Well fuck, neither do I!

"Are you going to spend the whole weekend not speaking to me?" he asks.

"No," I quickly answer.

"Good, because that would make things awkward for me."

Awkward? That would make it fucking awkward?

It takes all of my willpower not to talk back to him. I pick up my mug instead and sip my coffee.

"Why don't you go and freshen up and then we can spend the day watching films and cuddling on the sofa," he suggests, although I know it's not a suggestion, it's what he wants me to do.

"Okay." I stand up, taking my mug with me, and I turn to walk out of the kitchen.

"And don't even think about sneaking your phone in the bathroom with you. I have already taken the liberty of hiding it, just in case you feel the need to go contacting your friends."

I don't miss the smirk plastered on his face. I just nod and proceed to the bathroom.

The hurt that I am feeling is indescribable.

I thought that when he hit me that it was bad, but it doesn't even come close to the stabbing pain that is searing my heart.

Chapter Thirty-Two

NUMB

It's now five-thirty in the evening, and Michael has been acting like his old self since I emerged from the bathroom this morning. I'm so confused by his behaviour right now. How can he be so loving one minute, and a monster the next? It doesn't make sense.

Maybe I am going crazy?

Maybe I am at fault and I just can't see it?

"Which one do you want to watch next?" he asks me, getting up to take the DVD out of the DVD player.

"I don't mind, you pick."

"No, no, I insist."

"Something with action in it." There is no way that I want to be watching a romantic chick flick right now.

"Okay, well we either have Pulp Fiction or The Godfather."

"Pulp Fiction is fine."

"Pulp Fiction it is." He puts the film on and then comes back to the sofa, sitting as close to me as possible and putting his arm around me.

"This is nice," he comments, and all I can do is merely hum in agreement. "Are you okay?" he asks me. He must sense my discomfort.

"I'm just tired." I want to scream at him that no, I am not okay, and he is the reason why, but I daren't.

"Want to go to bed instead?"

"No."

I don't want to be in bed with him. He doesn't push the issue, but about five minutes into the film, he starts to nibble on my ear lobe. Any other time he has done this I have been more than willing to see where it leads, but today, I don't think I could muster up any sort of sexual feelings towards him.

"I'm not really in the mood," I say, hoping that he doesn't fly off the handle. He pauses for a beat before answering.

"Well, I guess it's my job to put you in the mood then, isn't it?" He resumes the nibbling and I bite down on my bottom lip, hard, to stop myself from crying. As he moves his lips to my neck, I remain silent.

Is this going to be my life now?

I can't let this happen.

I don't want him touching me.

"Honestly, Michael, I am way too tired to even think about getting in the mood." I gently brush him off me and edge my body away.

"Please yourself," he says as he sits back and focuses on the film once again. The tension returns, and I pray that Sunday passes by quickly.

I just want to get to Monday morning so that I can go to work and get the hell out of here.

Chapter Thirty-Three

WISHFUL THINKING

If I thought that being at work was going to give me a breather from Michael, I was sadly mistaken. He has somehow managed to convince Mr Collinson to allow him to work with Tyler and I on our joint project.

I could have screamed when Mr Collinson came to tell me the news. Instead of asking how the hell Michael managed to convince him, or how the hell I was supposed to bring Michael up to speed on everything, I just smiled. Fucking smiled. I have spent the whole day explaining the campaign to Michael, whilst Tyler has been sitting idly by because he needs me to work on the next part of the project with him. It has been a complete waste of a day as far as I am concerned.

"Can I take off?" Tyler asks, even though it isn't quite five o'clock yet.

"Sure," I say with a sigh.

"Thanks, boss." Tyler is up and out of here faster than a rocket. Can't say that I blame him as it hasn't exactly been easy to be in this room today. Sure, I have tried to act like my normal self, but even I can tell that I have been tense and awkward. Michael, however, has taken no notice and has had a smile plastered on his face all day long. He's smug about landing this opportunity. It means that he can keep a close eye on me. It means that I can tell no one. Just another way for him to keep fucking tabs on me.

"Hey, guys," Kim says, poking her head around the door. "Do you fancy grabbing a quick drink before going home? I've had a shitter of a day and need to unwind."

My eyes go to Michael as I know that if I answer then it will only piss him off.

"Sure, just a quick one though," he replies, and I feel relief surge through me that I won't have to go home alone with him just yet.

"Great, I'll just grab my things and meet you by the exit." Kim bounds away, and I start to pack away all of my paperwork.

"Lucy," Michael says, placing his hand on mine. I flinch and then curse myself for being so jumpy. Michael notices and has a genuine look of hurt on his face. I find myself feeling guilty about my reaction.

My head is screwed.

I'm the one feeling bad when it should be him on his hands and knees, grovelling for my forgiveness.

"We don't have to go if you would rather just go home."

"No," I answer a little too quickly. "No, it's fine, I would like to go for a drink and unwind." Michael nods and releases my hand, allowing me to continue gathering my stuff together.

We both walk out of the project room a minute later, and I go to my desk, putting all of the papers in my drawer. Michael takes my hand in his, entwining our fingers, and leads the way to the exit.

When we meet Kim, she is all smiles and chatter as we make the short walk to Alan's. I answer Kim when the need calls for it, but apart from that, I don't say much.

As we enter the bistro, Michael leads us to a booth and I slide in, Kim sitting opposite me.

"What do you ladies want to drink?" Michael asks.

"A large red wine, please," Kim answers.

"A small white would be nice."

"Be back in a sec," Michael says before walking over to the bar counter.

"Are you okay, Luce?" Kim asks me, concern etched on her face. "You look a little pale."

"I'm not sure if I'm coming down with something," I lie.

"Maybe you should go home and get yourself to bed?" Kim suggests.

"No." Once again, I answer too quickly, and Kim picks up on it straight away.

"What's really going on?" she asks, after staring at me for a few seconds.

"Nothing."

"Lucy, I know you, something is off."

"I'm fine," I answer quietly as I see Michael paying for the drinks and picking them up to bring over.

"No, you're not."

"Just drop it, Kim," I snap.

The last thing I want is for Michael to think that I am telling her anything. He comes walking over, his eyes zeroed in on me, and I force a smile on my face. Kim remains tight-lipped as Michael gives both of us our drinks and then slides in the booth next to me.

"So, how was your weekend?" I say to Kim, trying to make polite chit-chat.

"Um, it was good, once we left Jeremy's parents. We went out with Cal on Saturday night, and then Sunday was spent recuperating from the hangover." I feel a pang as she talks about going out with Cal. Normally, I would have been there with them. All three of my closest friends going out without me doesn't feel right.

"In fact, I tried calling you to see if you wanted to join us, but your phone just kept going to voicemail," Kim continues.

"That would be my fault," Michael pipes up before I can respond. "I'm afraid I kept Lucy chained to the bed all weekend." Michael chuckles away to himself as I feel embarrassed by his comment.

"You two are like a pair of randy teenagers," Kim exclaims with a smile on her face.

"What can I say, the honeymoon period is still very much alive," Michael says, putting his arm around me and placing a kiss on my forehead.

"How do you keep it so fresh and exciting?"

"We have our ways," Michael replies, his eyes locking with mine. I hear Kim say how sweet that is, and I plaster a smile on my face.

But inside, I'm dying.

I've never felt so helpless and uncertain.

I feel suffocated, alone, and afraid.

I'm not sure which is worse.

Chapter Thirty-Four

GOOD BEHAVIOUR

"You have been so good this week," Michael tells me, as if I am a child who has done as they have been told. "I guess my punishment last weekend worked a treat, huh?"

"I guess," I reply flatly.

"Well, as a treat, why don't we invite Kim and Jeremy round here for dinner tomorrow night?" he suggests.

"Sounds good."

"I mean, Kim has been going on about us all getting together again, but I don't really fancy going out. If we stay here, then we don't run the risk of bumping into anyone else." What Michael really means is that we won't run the risk of Cal coming along.

"Okay."

"Here," he says, pulling my phone out of his pocket and handing it to me. I look at him flabbergasted. He has kept my phone all week long, so I find it strange that he is giving it back to me now.

"I can have my phone?" Even I can hear how pathetic I sound.

"Of course," he says with a chuckle. "How else will you ask Kim and Jeremy to come round?"

"I just presumed that you would text one of them." He has both of their numbers, after all.

"I think it would be nicer if you invited them. I mean, it may look a little strange that I text Kim instead of you."

"Whatever you think is best," I reply as I take my phone from him and switch it on.

"I'll have it straight back after," he clarifies.

Of course he will.

How stupid of me to think that he would let me keep it.

The phone screen comes to life and instantly pings with several text messages. I am about to open the messages when Michael abruptly snatches the phone back off of me.

"I don't think that you need to be bothered with any of these," he says. "I'll just get rid of them."

"Please let me see them," I say without thinking. He pauses and looks at me, narrowing his eyes.

"Why? Who do you think they are from?"

"I don't know, but they may be important," I say in a quiet voice, wishing that I had just kept quiet in the first place.

"I don't think that anything Cal has to say is important," he replies before resuming his act of deleting the messages. His jaw ticks as he clearly reads them first, but there is no way that he can blame me for receiving a text message, can he?

"There," he says a few moments later. "All gone. Now you can text Kim." I take the phone back off of him and hold back the tears that threaten to emerge. I don't think that I have ever cried so much in all of my life, not even when Tom and I broke up. I send a quick text to Kim and then hand the phone back.

"I'll just leave this on to wait and see if we get a reply," he says, as if this is normal fucking behaviour.

"Okay."

"Why don't you go and have an early night? You look shattered and we don't want you looking anything but your best for tomorrow night now, do we?" He raises one eyebrow and I stand up like a good girl and go to the bedroom. I shut the door behind me, throw myself on the bed, and silently scream into the pillow.

My life isn't supposed to be like this.

I'm not meant to be controlled.

How did I let this happen?
How could I not see this coming?
Why do I feel so weak against him?
I need to find a way of escaping here, and quick.

Chapter Thirty-Five

FALSE PRETENCES

"I'm so glad that you both came here tonight," Michael says to Jeremy and Kim as we sit at the kitchen table after finishing the meal that I prepared for us all.

"Eh up, he's about to do a toast," Jeremy says, laughing.

"It must be serious," Kim chimes in.

"It is actually," Michael confirms. "I don't know if either of you realised, but today is the day of mine and Lucy's one year anniversary."

Fuck.

One year already?

It had completely slipped my mind, but that's hardly surprising with everything that has been going on.

"That's why we wanted you two here tonight, to celebrate with us," Michael continues.

"Ah, that's so sweet," Kim says, placing her hand over her heart.

Yeah, real fucking sweet.

Shame that he treats me worse than a dog.

"There's something that I have been wanting to ask for a while now," Michael says as he stands up and puts his hand in his trouser pocket. I stare at him with wide eyes as I anticipate what he is going to say.

"I think that it's fair to say that Lucy and I have had our ups and downs, but for the most part, we have been blissfully happy. I couldn't imagine my life without her in it, and I never want to. You complete me, Lucy. You were always the missing part of me. You made me come alive, learn to love, and my heart belongs to you." I hear Kim gasp, and my heart pounds faster with every word that comes out of his mouth.

Please don't do what I think you are about to.

Please just finish the toast by raising your glass.

Please God don't let him trap me further.

"On that note," Michael continues as he pushes his chair back and drops to one knee beside me. "I would be honoured if you would agree to spend the rest of your life with me." With those words, he pulls a small box out of his trouser pocket and opens it, revealing a silver ring with three small diamonds along the front.

"Oh my god," Kim says in the background, but I barely hear her over the rushing of the blood pumping in my ears.

"I love you, Lucy, and I want the whole world to know that you're mine." His eyes bore into me, and I know that he thinks this declaration is heartfelt, but I am feeling nothing but panic right now.

"I think that we make a great team, and I want to be able to call you my wife." He takes a deep breath and blows it out slowly before finishing his speech. "Marry me, Lucy, and I will spend the rest of our days making you happy."

Oh god.

I can't breathe.

I can't think.

I can't marry him.

I can't let him do this to me.

I don't want to spend my life with him.

I just want to get the fuck out.

His expectant eyes shine with unshed tears, and I can feel Kim and Jeremy holding back their excitement as they wait for my answer.

My mouth is dry, my hope of leaving dying as I utter the words that everyone else wants to hear.

"Yes."

Chapter Thirty-Six

NO WAY OUT

"We had a great night," Kim says as she kisses my cheek and takes one last look at the foreign object on my ring finger. "Damn, girl, that is pretty."

"It is," I say as I try to inject some life into my answer.

"We should do this again soon," Michael says as he comes up behind me and wraps his arms around my midriff.

"Definitely. Congratulations again, guys," Jeremy says before he opens the front door and walks out, Kim trailing behind him.

"See you Monday," she calls as they walk away.

I close the front door with a heart that feels like lead.

"Well, that was a success," Michael says, turning me in his arms and pushing me against the front door.

"What are you doing?" I ask as he starts to kiss my neck.

"I'm kissing my fiancée, what does it look like?"

"Can't we clean the place up first?" I am stalling. I don't want him to kiss me.

"The cleaning can wait, I, however, can't."

"But Michael—"

"Don't you want to please your husband-to-be?" he asks me, putting on a look of hurt.

"Of course I do, but—"

"Well then, get in the bedroom and show me how much you love me." I gulp down the lump that has formed in my throat and I make my way to the bedroom.

It's just sex.

I can do this.

Michael follows me and shuts the bedroom door behind him, bathing us in darkness.

I block my mind, feeling absolutely nothing as we have sex.

Michael gave up on my pleasure a long time ago, so once he's done, he rolls over and passes out beside me.

He didn't notice my body freezing from his touch.

He didn't notice that I was disinterested.

And he didn't notice the tears that fell from my eyes the whole time.

Chapter Thirty-Seven

UNRECOGNISABLE

I am a shell of my former self.

Pale.

Washed-out.

Miserable.

Fucked.

I have put on a good front, but when I am by myself, I can see the change.

My whole personality has changed, and inside my head I am at war.

My reflection stares back at me hauntingly.

"You need to cheer the fuck up," Michael says as he walks into the bathroom and stands behind me.

"I'm okay."

"Well tell your face that." His acid tongue has gotten worse over the last few days. It doesn't matter how nice I am to him, he just picks at any little thing that he can. "Most women would be pleased to have just gotten engaged to a man that adores them."

I can't help the scoff that escapes my mouth and I instantly feel the hairs on the back of my neck prickle.

"What was that?" Michael asks, stepping closer to me.

"Nothing." Luckily, he doesn't push the issue. I don't have the strength in me to fight him right now.

"You have five minutes and then we need to leave," he says, exiting the bathroom and leaving me in peace, if only for a few moments.

I apply some make-up, let out a deep sigh, and go to the kitchen, where Michael is waiting for me. I can feel his eyes scrutinizing me as I pick up my handbag and hook it over my shoulder.

"You ready?" I ask, trying to sound more cheerful than I feel.

"Why have you got all of that slap on your face?" he asks.

"Pardon?"

"Go and take it off."

"What?"

"You heard me, go and take it off. All of it." This is the first time that he has commented on the way that my face looks. I have only used nude eyeshadow, mascara, and a glittery bronze eyeliner.

"But... why?"

"Do you think that I want other men looking at you and thinking that they can get in your knickers?" He looks and sounds outraged. Anyone would think that I had used a trowel to put my make-up on. "I'm not having you showing me up at work by rolling in looking like a fucking slag."

"Michael," I exclaim, already envisioning that I am going to pay for this supposed faux pas later on tonight.

"Don't Michael me. Go. And. Take. It. Off." He says each word slowly, dangerously.

"But it makes me feel better." I can't let him take another thing away from me, even if it does seem trivial.

"Well, it doesn't make me feel better, and as my wife-to-be, that should be your only concern from here on out. Now, do as I say and don't take too long about it."

My shoulders droop and I place my handbag back on the table.

Nothing I say will appease him.

Nothing I do is ever right.

I make my way back to the bathroom and I start to take the

make-up off. I don't let myself cry, I think that I am too numb from everything to forge any kind of reaction.

When I'm done, I return to Michael, who has a smirk on his face.

"That's better." Satisfied, he announces that we can now leave, and I follow him, feeling another little piece of my soul die.

Chapter Thirty-Eight

BROKEN HEARTS

I'm sat at my desk, drinking a cup of coffee, when my work phone rings. Placing my cup down, I pick up the receiver and put on a polite, cheery voice.

"Lucy?" the voice on the other end of the phone says.

"Cal?"

Shit.

"Why are you calling me at work?" I ask, a little abruptly.

"Why aren't you answering your mobile? I've been trying to get hold of you for over a week now."

Shit, shit, and double shit.

"I… um… it's broken."

Liar, liar, pants on fire.

"Is that so?" Cal replies.

"Yep."

Keeping my answers to a minimum should enable me to cut this call short. I can't risk Michael overhearing me. His desk may be on the other side of the room, but if he thinks that there is something wrong, he will be over here like a shot.

"Then how come you can message Kim but not me? And how

come you didn't tell me that you had gotten engaged?" His questions throw me off guard.

"I've been busy." I have never been like this with Cal. I'm always open with him, so for me to keep this from him, it's going to raise his suspicions.

"Too busy to send a bloody text message or give me a quick call?" he asks incredulously.

"Sorry." It's like my default fucking response for everything nowadays.

"What's going on with you, Lucy? Why are you being like this?"

"Like what?" Feign ignorance and the problem may go away.

"Seriously? You need me to answer that?"

"Yes, I do." I don't, but I can't tell him the truth.

"You're different with me. You don't seem to want to spend any time with me, and now you're even ignoring me." He sounds hurt, and my heart breaks at the fact that our relationship is suffering.

"I'm the same as I always have been." It's ridiculous to say, but it's all I can come up with.

"Bullshit. It's Michael, isn't it?" My silence speaks volumes, and I bite my bottom lip, blinking rapidly to stop myself from crumbling. "Does he have a problem with me? With us?"

"There is no us," I whisper, feeling my heart sink a little more.

"Lucy, I love you, and you're the person closest to me." His words choke me. His sincerity hits me right at my core. "I don't want to cause problems for you, but, fuck, I miss you."

"I miss you too," I say before I can stop myself. I mentally kick myself for voicing what my mind was thinking.

"Then tell me what I can do to help fix whatever is going wrong between us."

Seconds tick by.

My heart hurts.

My mind clouds.

My guard goes up.

Protection. That's all I want, and I am the only person who can do that. No one else. Just me. I can't involve anyone in my torment, and I don't want to, either. Everyone else has their own lives to lead, and I won't be a burden.

"There's nothing you can do," I whisper before putting the phone down.

I look up to see Michael staring at me. I give him a little wave and resume sipping my coffee. Without even being aware of it, Michael has taken another piece of my life away from me. He's made me distance myself from Cal, the one person that I have always had by my side.

The one person that can heal me.

The one person that I can't have near me.

Chapter Thirty-Nine

A DANGEROUS GAME

It's lunchtime, and I feel more despondent than ever. My conversation with Cal is playing on a loop in my mind. I could have told him. I could have asked him to help me, but that wouldn't be fair. I got myself into a relationship with Michael, and I should be the one to get out of it.

The thought of telling Michael that we're over terrifies me. He's beyond controlling, and I have no doubt that he would make me leaving him as difficult as humanly possible.

"You coming out to get some lunch?" Kim asks me as she puts her jacket on and rounds her desk.

"No thanks, I've brought my lunch with me." Something that I never used to do. Another thing that has changed. Another way that Michael can keep me under his watch.

"Luce, we haven't been for lunch together in ages. Chuck your sandwiches in the bin and come get some real food."

"I can't. I need to do some more paperwork as I'm behind again." I'm not, but I use the excuse that I have repeated more than once over the past two weeks. Kim sighs and asks if I want her to grab anything for me, but I decline.

I watch her leave the office and I feel a pang of jealousy that she has freedom. A ridiculous thing to feel, but I can't help it.

In fact, I envy everyone that chooses to do what they want with their free time.

Free.

That word sounds like heaven. That word is what I crave. I clearly used to take it for granted.

"I need to pop out of the office," Michael says, distracting me from my thoughts.

"Okay."

"I won't be long. You're staying here, aren't you?"

"Yes. I have my lunch with me."

"Good." He walks off and out of the office, and I am the only person left on the main floor. It's a welcome relief to be alone after most of the office workers kept looking at me this morning. I'm guessing that is due to the fact that I look washed-out and paler than a fucking swan.

I feel self-conscious about the fact that Michael made me take my make-up off. It's like I have nothing to hide behind. No barrier.

I open up my sandwich bag and take a measly bite of my cheese sandwich. I don't taste it. Eating isn't high on my priorities right now, but I know that I need to do as much as possible to retain some semblance of normality.

The only thing that I seem to have control over is what and when I put food in my mouth. I'm guessing that Michael doesn't feel the need to control this aspect of my life, yet.

The office door springs open, surprising me so much that I drop my sandwich in my lap.

"Bollocks," I say to myself as I scoop up the food and place it on top of the sandwich bag that sits in front of me on my desk. I look up, ready to scold the person who made me jump, but my breath is taken away by the sight of Cal standing there.

Shit.

Fuck.

He can't be here.

Why is he here?

Michael can't see him.

I can't see him.

This is bad.

Bad, bad, bad.

I struggle to control my breathing as Cal rushes to my desk and kneels down in front of me.

"Lucy," he says softly, his hand reaching for my cheek. As his fingers brush against my skin, I jolt back.

"What are you doing here?" I say harshly.

"I needed to see you." I can hear the desperation in his voice and see it on his face. It almost breaks my fucking soul.

"Why?" I ask on a whisper.

"To make sure that you were okay."

"Well, now that you can see that I am perfectly fine, you may leave," I reply, my voice stronger than a second ago. I fold my arms across my chest and wait for him to go. He doesn't.

"I knew that things weren't right," he says, voicing his concern.

"You need to go," I say, my urge to get him out of here before Michael returns reaching new heights.

"Why?"

"Because you just do."

"You're scared." His comment is spot on. Damn him for knowing me so well.

"I'm not."

"Lucy, I have known you since we were at school together. I know when you're scared, and I know when you're lying."

"I'm not lying," I shriek, exasperated that he just won't get the fuck out of here. I feel sick.

"I'm not going anywhere until you tell me what is going on with you." His eyes are determined, fierce, passionate.

"Who do you think you are? You swan back into my life after buggering off for a year and a half and you expect everything to be the same as it was before?" I will say anything at this point in order to get him gone. It doesn't matter how cruel my words are, if Michael sees Cal, then I will be given a lesson in just how cruel life can really get. "Just go, Cal. I don't need a knight in shining fucking armour thinking he has to try and save me."

"No," he bites back, and I throw my arms in the air at his answer.

"Damn you, Cal Bailey!" It's not often I use his last name, but when I do, it normally means that I'm frustrated with him, and right now, I am beyond frustrated.

My eyes keep darting to the door.

My time is running out.

I take Cal's hands in mine, and I give them a little squeeze as I look him straight in the eye so that I can convey as much emotion as possible. "He can't see you here."

I don't need to tell Cal who it is that I am referring to. He knows. He knows me, and he knows that I am frightened. I was a fool to think that I could keep it from him.

"Why not?"

"Oh god, don't make this harder than it already is," I say as I bite down on my lip, hard.

"Just answer me and then I'll go." His hand returns to my cheek, and this time I don't pull away. His touch comforts me, and god do I need comfort in my life right now.

I take a deep breath and voice the words that have been kept inside for so long. "Because he'll hurt me."

I watch the colour physically drain from Cal's face, and I hate that I am the one causing that. I hate that I have become so pathetic and weak. I hate that I have let a man get into my head and take over my life.

"Leave him," Cal says, as if I haven't already thought about that a million times.

"I can't."

"Yes, you can," Cal urges, his eyes glistening.

"It's not that simple."

"Yes, it is. You can come and live with me, we can figure it out together." His words hold so much promise, but they're just words. False hope.

"It's no use. I can't go anywhere."

"Why the hell not, Lucy?"

"Because he loves me."

"He loves you?" Cal replies sarcastically.

"Yes," I answer as I feel my defences dropping. "He loves me which means that he'll never let me go, and I can't bring anyone else into this." The thought of Cal or Kim being involved in the shitty situation I have found myself in would make me feel worse than I do now. The guilt would eat me up.

"Love doesn't work like that, Luce." His voice is gentle, calming, but all it does is fuel the anger deep down inside of me. Cal Bailey is going to try and talk to me about love? I don't think so.

"And how the fuck would you know?" I say, the venom in my voice making him reel back slightly.

"I know what love is, but I'm starting to think that you don't," Cal responds, poking the fucking fire a little more.

"Oh really? Is your love the kind where you just up and leave? The kind where you get a little bit scared, so you decide to keep things at the friend-zone?" I want to slap myself as I say each word. They just come tumbling out with no thought for how this is going to affect our friendship, or how Cal is going to respond to the fact that I am basically admitting that he friend-zoned me all those years ago. Cal's eyes shimmer, regret visible in them.

"Lucy," he whispers my name as he reaches for my hand, but I push back on my chair to give me more distance from him.

"Just leave me alone, Cal. I don't need you, and I don't need your judgement. I'm a big girl and I can make my own decisions." My jaw is set firm. I will not cry. I will keep my emotions on lock down. I have to if I am going to survive this. "Just go, Cal."

A few more seconds tick by.

I feel like I am on a knife's edge.

I will Cal to go, walk out of here, forget all about me and the fucking mess that I have become.

"Fine," Cal says as he stands up and puts his hands in the pockets of his jeans. Relief floods through me. Michael won't see anything. There will be no punishment for me tonight.

"You know where I am if you change your mind," Cal says, and

I say the only thing that I can to extinguish the last look of hope in his royal-blue eyes.

"I won't."

He shakes his head and walks away from me, and possibly out of my life for good.

Chapter Forty

I CAN'T WIN

Kim walks into the office after lunch, a stony look on her face. She storms over to her desk and flops down in the chair, swivelling it to look at me. I keep my eyes on the computer screen to indicate that I don't need a tongue lashing from her, but she ignores that and surges ahead with what I already know is going to come out of her mouth.

"What the fuck is the matter with you, Lucy?"

"Nothing." I've had months of training to appear unaffected. There is no emotion to my voice.

"Bollocks. I've just spoken to Cal." This has me whipping my head around to her, my body going into panic mode.

"Do you have to shout?" I scold her, quickly looking across the room to Michael. Luckily, he seems to be engrossed in some chatter with the guy who sits at the desk behind him, so he has his back to me.

"Well, someone has to."

"Why?"

"Are you seriously asking me that? Do you need me to tell you that Cal is really upset?"

"I don't have time for this, Kim, and I don't want to talk about Cal."

"Well, I do." She folds her arms across her chest, and I know that she isn't going to back down. I need to wrap this conversation up quickly. "He came here to see you because you haven't bothered with him, and all you do is have a go at him."

"Is that what he said?" I ask, wondering how much Cal has told her.

"Not exactly, but I saw him leaving here, and I've never seen him so worked up in all the time that I've known him."

"Well, then he's being dramatic."

"We both know that Cal isn't dramatic, Lucy." Fuck. I'm screwed here. Kim has known Cal as long as I have, so she knows that he doesn't go in for dramatics, ever. "What is going on with you?"

"There's nothing going on," I reply adamantly.

"Oh come on, Luce, you don't call, you don't text, you don't want to hang out anymore or even go for lunch. And now you want nothing to do with Cal? There is something wrong and I'm not going to stop asking until you tell me."

"Well, you'll be waiting for a long time then because there is nothing to tell." I turn back to my computer screen, ending the conversation.

"Okay, fine," Kim says as she stands up. "If you won't tell me then I'll just go and ask Michael." She takes a step forward and I grab her arm in desperation.

"You can't ask Michael." I've already said too much with just that answer.

"Why?" Kim's eyes narrow, and I squirm in my seat.

"I... I..." And now I can see that Michael is looking over. I drop Kim's arm abruptly and look at her with pleading eyes.

"Please, Kim, I can't talk about it here, and I can't have Michael thinking that anything is wrong." Kim assesses me for a moment before sitting back at her desk. I breathe a sigh of relief, even though I can still feel Michael watching me from across the room.

"I want answers, Lucy."

"I know."

"We're going for a drink after work, no arguments."

I bite my bottom lip to stop myself from coming out with an excuse as to why I can't go with her. She won't take no for an answer now, and Michael will throw a fit when I tell him.

I can't fucking win.

Chapter Forty-One

SEPARATION

I am sitting in Alan's.

By myself.

On my own.

Well, technically Kim is at the bar getting us drinks, but still, there is no sign of Michael.

It's strange.

Almost surreal.

But fuck does it feel good.

He's not here, watching me, analysing me, breathing down my neck.

I haven't felt this relaxed in a long time. Sure, I'm going to get home and have to deal with the fallout, but for now, I am just going to enjoy having a drink with my friend.

Kim comes walking back over to our table and places a glass of white wine in front of me.

"Thanks," I say as she sits down and sets her beady eyes on me.

"Okay, let's get down to the nitty gritty. What is going on, Lucy? No bullshit," Kim says as she stares at me.

"Wow, talk about easing into a conversation," I say with a nervous laugh.

"We don't have time to ease into it. If what I think is true, then I imagine you have about an hour before you start getting all antsy and making excuses to go back home."

Jesus, has she climbed into my fucking brain to pluck that information out?

"And what do you think is the truth?" I ask, even though I am afraid to hear her answer.

Kim holds my gaze for a moment before speaking, and when she does, I feel like the air has been knocked out of my lungs.

"I think that Michael has some sort of control over you, and you are afraid to speak up. I think that he has changed you, and to start with I thought that was a good thing, but now I'm just worried about you." The sincere look in her eyes makes me want to burst into tears, but I manage to stop myself from showing her just how much of an emotional wreck I am.

"You don't need to worry, I'm fine," I insist.

"No, you're not."

"Michael just gets a little bit insecure sometimes."

"Really?" she says sarcastically with an eye roll.

"Yes. I guess he's just worried that I'm going to leave him."

"And why should he be worried about you leaving?"

"He shouldn't, and that's what I keep trying to tell him."

"Uh huh, and you think that's healthy?"

"What is this, Kim? Twenty questions?" I try to inject a little humour, but it just falls flat.

"This is concern. This is me wanting to help you."

"I don't need help."

"Does he hurt you?" Kim asks, completely knocking me sideways.

"What?" I say, whispering.

"Does he hurt you, Lucy?" Kim's expression is grim, and I am sure that mine is masked in horror. I look down at the table, desperately trying not to give anything away.

I can't tell her.

It's my problem, not hers.

I suddenly wish that I wasn't here having this drink, my joy at having a little freedom evaporating. If I had just gone straight home, then I wouldn't have been subjected to this line of questioning. I also wouldn't have the lurking thought of what Michael is going to do when I walk through the front door.

"Lucy," Kim says as she places her hand over mine. I look up at her and a lone tear slides down my cheek. "Does he physically hurt you?" Kim has the decency to talk quietly. I feel caged, as if I am being cornered.

This is my chance.

I can do this. I can tell her.

I can find my voice.

I open my mouth, ready to spill my secrets to her, when I hear him.

"Lucy," Michael says from the side of our table. I whip my head around and take in his form standing there, looking down at me. I feel any colour that I had left drain from my face.

I can't speak.

Why is he here?

Did he hear what Kim said?

Did he sense that I was about to break?

Did he come here to make it clear that I can never escape?

"Hey," I say as I hastily swipe my cheek, wiping away the wet trail left by my tear. "What are you doing here?" I put on a fake, cheerful voice and force a smile onto my face.

"I just came out to pick us up some food and thought I would drop in and see what you fancied," he says, his eyes intently searching mine.

"Oh."

"Are you okay?" he asks, his expression conveying sympathy. I just nod at him in reply. I can feel Kim watching us both as she sits quietly on the opposite side. The air around us is so tense that there is no way that it can go unnoticed.

Michael's jaw tenses, and I know that he doesn't believe me. He's wary.

"Um, actually, I don't feel too good," I say, hoping that this will suffice his overactive imagination.

"No?" He places his hand on the back of my head and I have to stop myself from flinching at his touch.

"My stomach's hurting."

"Maybe you should come home with me?" Michael suggests, and I can see Kim shake her head slightly in my peripheral vision.

"I think that's a good idea." I haven't even drunk any of my wine, but that's the least of my worries. "I'm sorry, Kim," I say, needing her to let me walk out of here without her asking questions. "I need to go."

"Sure," she replies, shocking the hell out of me with the one-word answer. I can see the disappointment in her eyes though, she doesn't need to tell me.

"I'll see you tomorrow?" I say as I shuffle off of the seat and into Michael's outstretched arm. As I step close to his body, he curls his arm around me, placing his palm on my shoulder, squeezing slightly. I gulp down the lump that has formed in my throat.

"Okay."

"Bye, Kim," Michael says before turning me around and marching me out of Alan's.

I can feel Kim's eyes burning a hole in my back as I walk away.

I feel sick, the nausea sweeping through me at a rapid pace.

When Michael gets me outside, he heads in the direction of the apartment.

"Did you not want to get food?" I ask, wanting to prolong the idea of being interrogated a little longer.

"I think it's best that we don't." His tone says it all. He's pissed, and I'm in trouble. He must have heard Kim to be this annoyed. His grip tightens more on my shoulder, but I don't squirm. If I squirm, he will only dig his fingers in more. So, I walk along, gritting my teeth and bearing the pain.

It turns out that in my haste to get some distance from Michael, I may have just fractured my friendship with Kim a little bit more.

Chapter Forty-Two

THE STORM BREWS

"I'm going to go and have a bath," I say as Michael and I enter the apartment. I don't wait for a response, I just want to get away from him and have some time to myself before I have to deal with his mood. He hardly spoke on the way home, and I know that he is working himself up. The sooner I am out of sight, the better.

I take my jacket off, hang it by the door, slip my shoes off and head for the bathroom. I start to run the bath, pouring a generous amount of bubble-bath into the water, enjoying the scent of roses as the water starts to bubble.

As I watch the water fill up the tub, I feel Michael stood behind me, and I can't help but let out a sigh.

It turns out that I'm not going to get the peace that I was craving a few seconds ago.

"What was Kim talking to you about at Alan's?" he asks me, going straight for the kill.

"Nothing much, we didn't really get to talking before I felt off and then you showed up."

"So it's my fault that your drinks were cut short?"

Oh for Pete's sake, he has to bring it back to him every single time.

"I didn't say that, Michael."

"You implied it."

"No, I didn't, you just took it the wrong way."

Lately, he seems to take everything the wrong bloody way.

The water gets to the level that I want it to, and I shut the taps off. I start to undress, all the while aware of Michael still stood behind me.

As I put my clothes into the washing basket, I plunge one foot into the water and my skin tingles from the heat. I immerse myself fully in the bubbles and sit back, closing my eyes and trying to ignore Michael's domineering presence.

It's hard to act relaxed when every single part of me is screaming to get the hell away from him and get the hell out of here.

My mind is a jumble of thoughts that are constantly warring with themselves.

He loves me.

He doesn't mean to get so angry.

He hurts me.

He makes me feel weak, helpless.

He makes me want to fight for what we used to have.

We were good together once, weren't we?

When did it all go so wrong?

We just need to work harder.

I need to behave better.

I need to stop pissing him off.

My thoughts are halted as my head is pushed until I am under the water.

My eyes fly open and immediately sting from the water and the bubbles.

I can make out an arm above me, a hand pushing me down. I struggle against Michael's overwhelming strength as I fight against trying to take a breath under the water.

Panic grips me.

Pain surges through me.

I lift my hands and bat at his arm as I yearn to taste the air. He doesn't budge.

I kick my legs, sending water flying everywhere.

I try to scream out, but it just comes out muffled. My heart pounds, my blood pumps.

He's got to let go.

He has to.

He can't do this to me.

It's my fault for angering him.

I should never have gone for a drink with Kim.

This is my fault.

I'm a bad girlfriend.

The thoughts continue to rage, my hands continue to hit out.

I lose the battle and open my mouth, an animalistic sound ripping from my throat. I can't fight this anymore. I don't have the strength. I can't even cry. All I can do is feel the pain in my lungs from holding my breath, and the pain in my heart that my world is crashing down around me just a little bit more.

I stop kicking.

I stop fighting.

I let my hands fall into the water.

I close my eyes.

I'm done.

Chapter Forty-Three

A WAKE-UP CALL

As my head is pulled out of the water, I splutter and gasp for breath. My arms grip onto the side of the bath, and I continue to cough. My eyes fly open, stinging from the air. My vision is blurry, and I feel light-headed.

I need to get out of this bathtub.

I try to pull my body up, but I feel weak. The shock of what just happened has made my blood run cold.

When I eventually get my eyes to focus, I look to Michael, who is towering over me, a grim expression on his face.

Minutes pass and I am still trying to regulate my breathing. My throat feels sore and is screaming at me to get a drink, but I daren't move.

Michael may have hit me before, but this is a whole new playing field.

"Christ," Michael says as he kneels down beside the bath, making me jump backwards, sending more water sloshing everywhere.

I don't want him near me.

I don't want him to touch me.

"Lucy, I'm so fucking sorry," he says as he places his hands on the side of the bathtub.

I sit, trembling. The water no longer feels warm and inviting. My teeth chatter as I continue to push myself back.

"I didn't mean to, I'm so sorry." His eyes may look genuine, but I've seen that look before. It's the look he gives me when he knows that he has gone too far. It's the look he does when he knows that he has got to up his game in the sorry stakes.

"Get away from me," I whisper, my throat hoarse.

"No," he replies with a shake of his head. "I'm not leaving you."

"I don't want you near me."

"But I love you, and I didn't mean to. I just get so mad sometimes that I do stupid shit." His excuse is just that, an excuse. It's not a reason for why he treats me like this. It's not good enough.

"Please go away," I whisper, my eyes wide, my heart beating a million miles a minute.

I don't want to talk, I don't want to listen. When I listen to him, he works his way into my mind. He plays games with me, and I can't let him continue to do that. I can't let him think that I am okay with this.

He reaches across the bathtub and my hands fly up in front of my face, and I let out a cry of alarm. He freezes, his hand just in front of me before he withdraws it and hangs his head in shame.

Quietly, he gets up and leaves the bathroom, shutting the door behind him.

My heart continues to hammer in my chest as I expect him to come crashing back in here. A few minutes pass before I am able to get myself out of the bathtub. The first thing I do is lock the bathroom door. I grab a towel and wrap it around my body before sitting on the bathroom floor. I bring my knees up, wrapping my arms around them. Tears spill down my cheeks. I'm angry, sad, disappointed, pained, frightened. My faith in relationships has taken a serious knock since I've been with Michael.

I have spent months turning a blind eye or giving into him and believing his excuses for why he behaves in the way that he does. I have given him the benefit of the doubt because I thought that he loved me, but I can see now that he doesn't love me in the way that he should.

His love for me is terrifying.

He wants me all to himself, and he wants me to obey him.

He wants to control me, and I have let him do just that for most of our relationship without realising it.

This moment has given me a wake-up call.

This moment has flipped a switch inside of me.

I will forever remember this moment as the moment that I decided to leave Michael.

I need to get out.

I need to save myself.

Chapter Forty-Four

WALKING AWAY

After getting dried, putting some clothes on and towel-drying my hair, I walk into the kitchen with a new determination in me.

I don't want to be scared anymore.

I want to be the person that I once was.

As I look to the lounge, I see Michael sat on the sofa, his head hanging in shame.

Good. He deserves to feel ashamed of what he has done to me.

There is a small part of me that does feel sorry for him, but I slap the feeling away as quick as it comes. I don't want any guilt to consume me. If I even let a slither of it in, then I am going to be a goner.

"I want my phone," I say, my voice rock solid for the first time in months.

The tension in the apartment radiates around me, but I won't lose focus. I need to get out of here. Michael keeps his head hanging when he answers me, so I have to strain my ears to hear his muffled answer.

"It's on top of the wardrobe."

With purpose, I turn and go back to the bedroom, standing on the bed so that I can peer on the top of the wardrobe. There, at the front, sits my phone and charger. I grab both things and turn my phone on once I have safely stepped down from the bed and back onto the floor. I expect my phone to be dead, but as the screen comes to life, I can see that it is nearly at full battery. I suspect that Michael has been keeping watch on who messages me and what they say.

My phone vibrates a few seconds later, and I see that I have a few missed calls from Kim, all from this evening, after I left Alan's. I also have missed calls and texts from Cal.

My heart hammers as I open the texts from him and read through them.

> Lucy, I didn't mean to upset you earlier. I hope that you can forgive me and we can repair our friendship. Please give me a call so we can talk. Cal x

> Luce, I don't want to lose you. You have been my best friend since we were younger. I love you, and I just want to make this right. Don't let my behaviour ruin what we have. Cal x

My heart breaks as I picture Cal writing those messages. I know that my reaction to him earlier would have crushed him. It crushed me, but he has no idea that I was just trying to protect myself. He has no clue about what I have been going through—no-one does.

I wasn't ready to admit it before, but I am now. I'm ready to acknowledge that I need to get out of this abusive relationship with Michael before it's too late.

I put my phone in my pocket and go back to the kitchen, placing my charger in my handbag. Michael still hasn't looked up, and I would rather that he didn't. He might be hurting, but so am I, and I need to think of myself for a change.

"I'm going to stay somewhere else," I say, my tone firm and unwavering. Still no response. "I will come and pick up my things in a few days' time."

I can hear him sniffle, but I force myself to turn away and walk out of here. I need to piece my life back together, and I can't do that with him near me.

As I open the front door and walk out, I let out a cry of relief.

He let me walk away.

I showed him that I don't need him.

I can allow myself to breathe again.

Although I am feeling a weight being lifted from my shoulders, my heart still drops lower in my chest. That's how much he has messed with my emotions.

Michael is done fighting for me, and I'm done fighting for him.

I need to be strong, and I need to realise that this is the beginning of the end.

Chapter Forty-Five

BLURRED REALITY

I knock on the door in front of me and wait.

Seconds tick by as I stand there, with just my handbag. I didn't pack any of my stuff, I just wanted to get the hell away from Michael. I hear laughter from behind the front door, and I realise that I am probably intruding. I turn away and walk down the path, opening the front gate and closing it behind me. I look left and right, the street completely deserted as I contemplate my next move.

I have no idea where to go. Kim's would be the obvious choice, but I can't deal with all of her questions right now. She would bombard me, and all I really need is somewhere to lay my head and process what has happened.

As I am about to head right and walk into town, I feel a hand on my shoulder. The scream that comes out of my mouth is piercing. I drop my handbag and it lands with a thud on the floor. I crouch down, cowering. My whole body shakes as my brain tells me that Michael has followed me. He's come here to finish what he started back at the apartment.

My hands are over my ears, my eyes are closed, and I start to rock on my heels, backwards and forwards, backwards and forwards.

I mentally prepare myself for the fist that is surely coming my way.

"Lucy."

"No," I whisper as tears stream from my eyes. I thought that he had let me walk away. I thought that he had realised that he had gone too far.

"Lucy." The deep voice is insistent, urgent.

A hand is placed on my back lightly, and far too gently for it to be Michael.

I stop rocking and open my eyes.

"Hey, it's okay."

It takes me a few more seconds to register that it is Cal speaking to me, not Michael. I look at his face as he crouches beside me, and I can see the worry in his eyes. "It's just me, Luce."

"Cal," I say on a breath.

"Yeah, babe, it's me."

"Cal," I repeat as I suddenly move and wrap my arms around his neck. He doesn't pry me off of him as my tears dampen his shirt. He manoeuvres us so that we are both standing before wrapping his arms around me and holding me close to him.

His closeness is such a comfort after months of feeling on edge. I have missed him so much. Our bond is special, and I worry that Michael has broken what we once had.

Cal doesn't rush me as my body racks with sobs. I guess I am crying for a multitude of reasons. Hurt, anger, stupidity, disappointment, relief, the list could go on.

"I've got you," Cal says as he loosens his grip and picks me up so that I am cradled in his arms. He doesn't turn me away, but instead picks my handbag up off of the floor and carries me up the path and into his house. I feel him kick the door shut behind us.

"Everything okay, Cal?" a deep voice booms to my left. My fingers curl into Cal's shirt at the sound of another man's voice.

"I'll just be upstairs in my room," Cal replies, holding me just a little bit tighter.

"Okay, dude."

I can't look up to acknowledge the man that Cal has been

talking to. If he thinks that I am rude then so be it. I don't want to speak to another man right now, I just want to be with Cal. He's my rock, my saviour, my world.

Cal carries me up the stairs and to his room. I hear him click the door shut behind us when we have reached the relevant room.

He doesn't speak, and for that I am grateful. I don't know how I would explain my meltdown to him whilst still sobbing like the broken woman that I am.

I feel him lean down, and I come into contact with a soft mattress. Turning on my side, I shuffle forwards and feel Cal lay down behind me. His arms hold me as his chest presses against my back. I don't push him off, he makes me feel safe. He always has done, and he has always known exactly what I need.

Chapter Forty-Six

TRUTH

I struggle to open my eyes as they feel sore and swollen. I rub them gently, the rawness of all the crying that I did last night making them tender to touch.

As I open them slowly, they drift to the empty space beside me. Cal had been there when I had cried myself to sleep last night, but now there is just an empty space. My hand drifts over to the emptiness, tracing the creases in the sheet from where he lay.

I don't know what I would have done if it hadn't been for Cal. He is a part of me, always has been and always will be.

I close my eyes and rub my temples as a dull ache pulses in my head.

"Good morning," I hear Cal say, making me open my eyes abruptly to see that he is walking into the room with a couple of mugs in his hand. He closes the door behind him and walks over to the bed, passing me one of the drinks. I prop myself up against the headboard and take it from him.

"Thanks," I say as I breathe in the scent of the coffee.

"How are you feeling this morning?" he asks as he sits down on the bed, facing me.

"I'm okay," I say with a shrug of my shoulders.

"I don't think so, babe," Cal replies with one eyebrow raised. "Are you going to tell me what happened last night?" His eyes hold mine, and I find that I want to tell him. Hell, I probably need to tell someone for my own sanity.

"I... I left Michael."

Cal splutters on the mouthful of coffee that he is taking.

"As in, for good?" he asks, leaning over and placing his cup on the bedside table. I nod my head, the tears wanting to emerge again.

Surely, I can't cry any more than I already have?

I take a deep breath, rapidly blink the tears away and begin to talk.

"Things have been a bit tense for a while now, and I just can't stay with him. When we first started dating, it was fun, exciting, and a welcome distraction from being miserable from what Tom put me through." I take a sip of my coffee, as my mouth has gone dry, before continuing.

"Michael used to be kind, caring, thoughtful. I honestly thought that I had found someone who wanted me just for me. Someone who wouldn't try to change me or get embarrassed by me, you know?" Cal nods his head but stays quiet. "I guess that, even though I loved Tom, I always felt a bit too dowdy for him."

"You have never been dowdy, Luce."

"Maybe not to you, but it's how I felt."

"Why didn't you say anything?"

"Because I always told myself that I was being silly, insecure, needy. I voiced my feelings to Tom once, but he just brushed them aside and I never mentioned it again. Then, when I found him and Carley together, I hit an all-time low. It confirmed what I thought about myself. I wasn't good enough, pretty enough, refined enough. Anyway," I say with a wave of my hand. "Michael made me feel different. He made me feel as though I was the only person that mattered. He made me feel good, Cal, really good."

The memories of our first few months together flood my brain. I close my eyes as I allow myself a moment to remember how good it was.

"So, what went wrong?" Cal interrupts me, his voice quiet and concerned. I open my eyes and take a deep breath. I need to get this out. I need him to try and help me understand what I did wrong.

"I don't know exactly, but Michael started to behave differently when I moved in with him. Not straight away, it was gradual. It was so fucking gradual that I never saw it coming. I never thought that I would be put in that position. How someone who was meant to love you could hurt you so much."

"What did he do?"

"He…" The idea of saying it chokes me. My throat feels like it is closing up.

Admitting this to another person is going to make it all the more real. I have spent months trying to hide it, so as much as I need to tell Cal, I'm also aware that voicing it will be a confirmation of sorts.

"It's okay, take your time," Cal says softly.

I look at him and let a small smile play on my lips. He moves closer and sits directly in front of me, his legs crossed, just like mine are. He takes my hands in his and holds them, rubbing his thumbs over my knuckles. It's soothing.

"He didn't like me going out without him. I just put it down to his insecurities, so I didn't allow myself to dwell on it too much. I figured that it was my place to show him that I wasn't going anywhere. Sometimes it worked, and other times it didn't."

Other memories flood my mind, and none of them are good. The feel of his hand on my face, the force with which he kicked me, punched me, the hateful words.

"He… He got so angry with me, told me that I wasn't behaving as a girlfriend should." My heart is starting to pound as I relive it. I haven't even been away from him for twenty-four hours yet, and my heart still hurts.

"He would say cruel things to me, make me feel worthless, but he would always explain why it was my fault that he had reacted in such a hurtful way. My mind was convinced that it was all my doing. I needed to change. I needed to be better."

"Lucy," Cal whispers, and I can hear the strain in his voice, the pain that he is feeling along with me. The tears can no longer be stopped, and they fall down my face as I fight to get the words out.

"The first time he hit me, I walked out, went to Kim's." Cal gasps, but I ignore it and carry on speaking—if I don't then I won't get everything out.

"He came to find me, told me he was sorry, it wouldn't happen again, and I believed him. I loved him, so why wouldn't I forgive him? He was okay for a short while, but then he hit me again. That along with his words made me scared, fearful. I pushed you and Kim away. He made me feel like I couldn't tell anyone, and I just kept making excuses for his behaviour. I dreaded anyone asking me to do anything because I knew that it would set Michael off. He was the one who took my phone away so that I had limited contact with you. He didn't like you in my life, that was obvious, but again, I tried to excuse it. Put it down to the fact that most guys would feel a little insecure about our close bond."

Cal's jaw is clenched tight, but I continue to get the words out.

"I never wanted to lose you, but I didn't want to piss Michael off further, so I chose the cowardly option. Instead of standing up to him, I allowed him to take over aspects of my life. He even managed to get himself on my project at work because he didn't like that I was working with Tyler." I scoff at how ridiculous this all sounds.

How could I have been so naïve and stupid?

"Last night, he tried to drown me as I took a bath. He held me under the water as I tried to get him off of me." My whole body is trembling now, and Cal has my hands gripped in his.

"I think he frightened himself at how far he had gone. I knew then that it was over, that I had to get out. I thought I was going to die, Cal, I really thought that he was going to kill me."

Cal lets go of my hands and moves me so that I am embraced in his arms. He holds me, just as he did last night. It feels good to tell someone, but fresh pain surges through me because the relief of telling someone also brings with it a burden that I may have just changed their opinion of me.

I don't want Cal to view me differently, and I now see that I have so much left to battle and no energy left to fight.

Chapter Forty-Seven

RECUPERATION

Cal spends the day looking after me. I have been lying in bed all day, watching films with Cal right by my side.

After telling him about what has been going on with me all these months, I guess he just wanted to try and help me relax, feel safe.

We hear the doorbell ring and Cal jumps up, grabbing his wallet from the bedside table.

"That's the pizza," he says, as if it wasn't obvious, seeing as we ordered food about half an hour ago.

I pick up the remote control and pause the DVD that we have been watching as Cal bounds from the bedroom.

I look to the ceiling, feeling a mixture of emotions, much as I have done for months now. The main feeling though is feeling safe. Michael can't get to me here. He doesn't even know where Cal lives, and I thank God that I never told him.

A few minutes go by and Cal still hasn't returned with the pizza. With my stomach grumbling, I push myself off of the bed and pad out into the hallway.

As I near the top of the stairs, I can see that Cal has his arms folded. I descend the first step when the next voice to speak makes my blood run cold.

"Please can I see her?"

Michael.

He found me?

How the fuck does he know that I am here?

"You're going nowhere near her," Cal says, and I can hear the determination in his voice. I hastily step back and hide behind the wall, keeping my ear pricked so that I can hear what is going on as I try to calm my racing heart.

"Why the hell not?" Michael asks, keeping his innocent façade in place.

Cal scoffs. "Are you seriously going to stand there and make out that you're innocent?" Cal says, and I hold my breath, waiting for Michael's response.

"Look, I don't know what she has told you about what has gone on, but she's not in her right state of mind. She's been behaving oddly for months now. I'm worried about her," Michael replies.

The sheer anger that I feel as I hear Michael speak each word is indescribable, and if I weren't so scared of what he might do, then I would march right down there and tell him what I thought of him. If only I wasn't such a coward.

"Please don't try and patronise me," Cal says. "I've known Lucy since we were kids, and I believe every single word that she has told me, so nothing you say will make a blind bit of difference."

I risk peering around the wall and see that Cal's jaw is clenched as he holds his defiant stance.

"You still have a thing for her, huh?" Michael says, his tone changing to add in more of an edge. Cal laughs at his question.

"Only someone with your mentality would ask me a question like that. I don't need to explain myself to you, and neither does Lucy."

"I knew that you didn't like me from the word go, and now you have made Lucy push me away."

"Michael, I don't have time for this."

"Why? You too busy fucking my fiancée?" Michael sneers, and I cover my mouth, disgusted at how vulgar his words can be. "LUCY!" he starts to shout, and my whole body convulses.

Cal won't let him in here.

No need to panic.

No need to be afraid.

It's easy to say those words inside of my head, but actually putting them into action is another matter entirely. Of course I'm going to panic, and of course I'm afraid. Who wouldn't be?

I breath in through my mouth and back out again, slowly, to try and regulate my racing heart.

"You are, aren't you?" Michael continues, and I sink to the floor, my knees pulled up in front of me, my head resting back against the wall as I try to keep focused on my breathing.

"You can think what you like," Cal retorts, which is going to do nothing to dampen Michael's temper. "Lucy and I are friends, good friends, and nothing will ever change that."

"Everything was fine until you came back. Lucy and I were happy, excited for our future, but the minute you showed your face everything changed. She changed. You changed her." Michael is on one, and I know that this is just the start. This is just him building until he loses it. "You ruined what we had together."

I peer around the wall again and see that Michael has come into view and is standing near enough nose-to-nose with Cal.

My heart thumps and all thoughts of regulating my breathing have gone. Cal doesn't look fazed in the slightest, but I am petrified that Michael is about to hurt my oldest and bestest friend.

"I didn't do anything, Michael."

"You fucking did," Michael says as I see him shove Cal. Cal stumbles back slightly, but not as much as I would have had Michael shoved me. "You should have stayed away. You didn't need to come back."

"Get out," Cal says, but I know that it will take something more for Michael to leave.

"I'm going nowhere until I have spoken to *my* fiancée." He advances towards Cal again, and I can see his hands are clenched into fists. I can't let him hurt Cal. I won't let Cal take a hit for me.

Before I can stop myself, I move on shaky legs down the first few steps. Neither of the men notice me to start with, so I walk down a couple more. Michael spots me before Cal does, and his focus shifts. Cal is no longer his target, I am. I walk to the bottom step and Michael starts to come towards me, but Cal beats him to it.

"It's okay, Cal," I say as Michael's eyes turn thunderous.

"He's going nowhere near you," Cal says, his gaze firmly fixed on Michael.

"I don't think that's your choice," Michael says, his teeth gritted.

I hate that I am in this situation. I shouldn't have to hide from a man that was supposed to love and cherish me. I shouldn't have to fear my friend getting involved.

"Lucy," Michael starts. "Please, baby, can we talk?" Nice Michael is back. He can change in a split second, and I wonder how he manages it. I certainly couldn't.

"I don't think that's a good idea," I reply, my voice quiet. I desperately want to cower down so that Cal hides me, but I don't. I need to do what I can to get Michael out of here.

"I'm sorry that things got so heated last night, I just want to work this out. I love you, Luce. I don't want to lose you." Words that I have heard before. Words that once filled me with hope, but now I know that they mean nothing. They hold no truth. "Just come home with me."

At one time, I wouldn't have hesitated to follow his silent order. I would have put on a front and let him take hold of my hand and take me home, but not this time.

"I'm not coming back."

"What?" He looks truly panicked, and I have to avert my eyes so that I don't get sucked into his mind games again.

"She said that she's not coming back," Cal says, reiterating the message.

Coming from behind Michael, two guys walk in, but stop in their tracks when they see that we have a stand-off going on.

"Everything okay?" one of the guys asks.

"Yeah," Cal replies. "Michael, here, was just leaving."

I can see that Michael is extremely pissed that this is not going his way. His jaw ticks, his hands twitch, and his breathing deepens.

"I'm coming back for you, Lucy. We can work this out," Michael says before throwing Cal a dirty look. He then turns around and marches out of the front door, past the other two guys, slamming the door behind him.

"What was all that about?" the second guy asks, his Irish accent thick.

"Nothing to worry about, lads," Cal says, and I am grateful for his secrecy in the matter. I let out a shaky breath and place my hand on Cal's shoulder to steady myself.

"You okay?" Cal asks me as he places his hand on mine.

"I think so." No. No, I'm not okay, but I've already burdened Cal with too much.

"You look a little pale."

"Just shocked more than anything. How the hell did he find out where you live?" I say, more to myself than to anyone else.

"You never told him?" Cal asks.

"No."

"I have no idea, but he isn't going to let you go easily."

"That's what I was afraid of." I look up to see that the two guys have disappeared, probably into the lounge. Another knock at the door has me jumping out of my skin. Cal goes and opens the door, clearly ready to face round two, but he starts to smile a few seconds later.

"Pizza's here," he says, turning to me, his smile easing my tension slightly. Cal pays the delivery guy and takes the pizzas.

"Come on," Cal says as he closes the front door and walks up to me. "Let's get back into bed, finish watching our film, and not talk about Michael."

People may not understand mine and Cal's relationship, but it works for us, and I wouldn't be without him.

"That sounds great."

Chapter Forty-Eight

NORMALITY

Three days have passed since I left Michael. Three days in which I have remained at Cal's, holed away from the outside world.

Cal is helping me to try and heal my broken heart and soul, but I am still all over the place. One minute I'm relieved, the next I'm miserable. There is no in-between right now.

I am currently sat at my work desk, watching the door like a hawk. Cal tried to convince me that I shouldn't be going anywhere, but I feel the need to try and get some semblance of normality back in my life.

After calling Kim last night and giving her a brief rundown of the last few days, she assured me that Michael hadn't been into work either. She just assumed that we both had a sickness bug of sorts, and although she had tried my mobile phone, I have kept it turned off.

It's nearly nine o'clock, and most of the staff have arrived. Cal made sure that he escorted me to my desk, and he assured me that he would be here to pick me up and take me back to his tonight. I tried to wave him off, but he was having none of it. To be honest, I am so glad that he hasn't gotten sick of me yet. He really has been the one that has held me together, and he has stopped me from returning to Michael when my mind just wanted to focus on all of the good times.

That's the problem, you see—my mind wants to block out the bad. Even my own brain wants to conspire against me.

"Hey, you," Kim says as she gets closer to my desk.

"Hey," I reply with a genuine smile on my face.

"How have you been? You don't look too good."

"Gee, thanks for that," I reply sarcastically, but with a chuckle so that she knows that I am joking.

"You sure that you should be back at work?" She gives me a concerned look, but I need her to understand that I need distraction.

As wonderful as Cal has been, it doesn't stop my brain from going over everything that has happened.

"Yes, I'm fine, and I am even more fine that Michael isn't here. I think that I would have stayed away had I known that he was still coming in," I reply, relief surging through me that it is now just after nine and there is still no sign of him. He would never be late to work if he was going to appear, so I can allow myself to relax and catch up on my workload.

"You know that I'm still mostly in the dark about what has been going on with you. Can we catch up after work, properly?" Kim asks me, her face looking hopeful that I will bring her more into the loop.

"Sure. Cal is meeting me when I finish, so we could go back to his and crack open a bottle of wine?" I suggest.

"I am so down for doing that," Kim replies as she gets settled at her desk and switches her computer on.

I smile and pull my phone out of my handbag to send a quick text to Cal, to let him know that I have invited Kim over later. He won't mind, it's something we used to do all the time before he went away.

I put my phone back in my handbag and am about to ask Kim if she wants me to make her a coffee, when I freeze. A cold feeling washes over me, the hairs on my neck standing to attention. My eyes flicker towards the main entrance of the office, and there stands Michael, his gaze fixed on me.

I suck in a sharp breath, my lungs suddenly feeling like they are closing up.

"Shit," I hear Kim say from her desk, but that word is putting it mildly.

I guess my day isn't going to be as relaxed as I thought it would be.

Chapter Forty-Nine

FRONTING IT OUT

I watch as Michael goes over to his desk and takes his jacket off. The sight of him has my adrenaline pumping. Michael scares me, and I bet the look is written all over my face.

As he puts his jacket on the back of his chair, my heart pumps wildly.

Please leave me alone.

Please don't make a scene at work.

Please, please, please.

I am disgusted with myself that I have become so pathetic. I thought that Tom cheating on me had been the most pathetic moment of my life, but I was wrong. Nothing compares to how I am feeling now.

I may not be the most outspoken person in the world, but I have never been so scared to voice my feelings or opinions before. I'm ashamed that I have let a man bring me down this much.

I take a few deep breaths, trying to calm the storm raging within me. A part of me wants to scream, shout, let everyone know what Michael has done. But I know that I won't do that. I don't need to make myself a target for pity and sympathy. I don't want anyone apart from Cal and Kim to realise what I have been through. It would be far too embarrassing.

"Lucy," Tyler's voice says, making me jump. I didn't even notice him making his way over to my desk as I was so focused on watching what Michael was doing.

"Shit," I whisper, my hands clenching into fists as I try to get a grip of myself.

"Sorry, boss, didn't mean to scare you," Tyler says as I look to him and see that he has a small but unsure smile on his face.

"No, it's fine, my fault, I was miles away," I reply, as I try to pass off my over-reaction. "What's up?"

I fiddle about with a couple of pens that are lying on my desk, just so that I can look at something other than Michael. I know that he is watching me, I can feel it. The hairs on the back of my neck prickle, and I start to feel a little hot.

"I was just going to see if you wanted to come and see what I have done in the last couple of days on our project? With you and Michael out of the office, I carried on getting the presentation in order."

"Oh, right, yes, presentation," I waffle, my mind a jumble of thoughts. "Uh, sure, let's go and look at it now."

"Cool." Tyler clearly has no idea that I am struggling, and for that I am glad. At least he isn't treating me any differently than he usually does.

I stand up, even though my legs feel shaky, and I follow Tyler to the conference room. He explains how he has it all set up and he is hoping that he has captured the vision that I was going for, but I barely take in what he says as Michael's eyes follow me across the room.

We have to walk past his desk to get to the conference room, and every bone in my body wants me to turn around and run away, but I can't. I need to work.

I stupidly let my eyes connect with his as I reach his desk. His eyes are hard, cold. A shiver makes its way up my body, and I wrap my arms around myself as a form of protection. But my body isn't the issue here. Unfortunately, the issue is my heart, and I have no idea how to get Michael out of it. He may have treated me badly, he may have hurt me, upset me, made me feel worthless, but my stupid goddamn heart can't just stop loving him.

Why can't I just hate him?

Why can't I just ignore him?

Is this part of his game? Make me love him no matter what?

"Lucy," he says as I pass his desk. I should keep walking, I should just march right past and forget him, but I don't. I stop, even though my head is screaming at me to show him that he can't control me.

"Lucy, look at me." He says it quietly enough so that no one else can hear around us, but I don't miss the command in his tone. And of course, I look at him. Good little girl that I am, not wanting to upset him or make anyone else think that there is anything wrong between us. I felt strong with Cal by my side the other night, but Cal isn't here now, and I revert to my old ways.

"We need to talk," he says, as if we have just had some meaningless lover's tiff.

"We're at work, Michael, we can't talk here," I whisper, keeping my face as neutral as possible.

"Tonight."

"I can't."

"Why not?"

"Lucy?" Tyler has realised that I'm not behind him anymore and has called my name in question.

"Yeah, I'm coming," I say, grateful for the interruption.

I can see that Michael is livid as I scurry away. Tyler's timing was perfect. I dodged Michael's questioning, and there is no way that he will be able to question me later, seeing as I will be with Cal and Kim.

Tyler and I enter the conference room, and I allow myself to breathe a sigh of relief. All I have to do is sit here and see what Tyler has come up with. Simple, work-related, and just what I need to distract my mind.

I take a seat at the end of the conference table as Tyler walks over to the projector at the other end of the room and starts to set it up. I sit back, feeling my heart-rate decline with each second that passes. Michael doesn't have a good effect on me, I know that, and I need to keep that feeling with me when my heart decides it wants to have a wobble and send me straight back to him.

"Right," Tyler starts as he flicks the projector on and the first slide shows up on the white screen, which nearly covers the wall. "So, I took on board what—"

"Get out." I whirl around in my seat at the sound of Michael's voice. The door bangs into the wall, just showing the force in which he opened it with.

"Sorry?" Tyler says, clearly confused by what is happening.

"You will be if you don't get out of here."

"Michael," I say, appalled and astounded that he has barged in here.

"What's going on?" Tyler asks.

My eyes are fixed on Michael, so I have no idea what expression is written on Tyler's face.

"I need to speak to Lucy, alone."

"Um, Lucy?" Tyler says, clearly asking me what he should do.

Michael's eyes bore into mine, and I know that if I don't do this now then it will only make things worse in the long run. I do the only thing that I have done throughout my entire relationship with Michael. I cower.

"Just go, Tyler, we won't be long."

"Oh, okay. Shall I come back in about five minutes?" Tyler asks.

"We'll come and get you when we're done," Michael answers before I have a chance to. He doesn't want just five minutes with me.

"Right." I watch as Tyler walks to the door and leaves the room, the sound of the door shutting behind him seeming to echo all around me. There is a blind on the door, which Michael pulls down before locking the door, trapping me in here with him.

Oh shit. I'm in so much trouble.

It's the last thought that I have before a searing pain radiates through my skull and I black out.

Chapter Fifty

I'M IN HELL

I hear a pounding.

It hurts my ears.

A voice screaming, shouting my name.

I try to call out but my mouth fills with vomit, stopping me from responding.

I turn my head to the side and empty the contents of my mouth.

The smell is acrid, the taste is vile.

My eyes are closed, and I battle to open them.

My head hurts. The pain searing.

"Lucy, Lucy, wake up." A panicked voice, someone's breath tickling my ear lobe. "Lucy, baby, please wake up."

I try to tell the person that I can't, but still my voice won't work. My lips can't form the words that they need to.

"I'm so sorry, Lucy. I love you, don't ever forget that I love you. Everything that I have done is for you."

I want to ask questions, get answers to the confusion that is swirling around my brain.

My eyelids begin to flutter, but a slither of light hits my eyes and I cry out. It's too bright. I squeeze my eyes back together, shutting myself in darkness.

I feel a hand stroke mine, it's touch gentle, as if it is trying to soothe me.

"Please, baby, I didn't mean to do it. I didn't mean to cause you so much pain. I just want you to love me. I need you to love me. Without you, I am nothing."

My heart beats at a steady pace.

My mind stops wondering what is going on.

"Wake up." The voice speaks more urgently, and I try to obey, I really do, but it's no use. I just want to sleep. I feel content, and I need to hold on to that feeling.

I just need peace.

I just want out.

It's time to give up my fight.

Chapter Fifty-One

REALITY SUCKS

Opening my eyes is excruciating. The light hurts and my head pounds.

I raise my hands up and place them either side of my head, needing to try and stop the thumping that is making me feel sick. I let out a groan and will myself to stop being a baby. I don't even register where I am until I hear a door open, the sound of the click alerting me, making me turn in the direction of the noise.

"Hi," he says, making my blood run cold. He walks farther into the room and shuts the door behind him. I glance around quickly, and a blinding pain hits. I cry out, and seconds later I feel the bed dip beside me where Michael has sat down.

"Don't make any sudden movements. You've had a bit of an accident."

An accident? The memory of the last time I was with Michael comes flooding back to me.

I was at work.

Michael barged in, interrupting me and Tyler.

I was on my own with him.

It only took a few seconds for him to hit me.

A hit to my head that knocked me out.

I can still hear the voice of Kim screaming from beyond the closed door.

I want to close my eyes and open them again only for this to be a fucking nightmare. I try it. He's still there. I'm not imagining it, it's all real. Fear spikes its way through my body. I need to get out of here, I need to be as far away from him as possible.

"I can see your mind working overtime, Lucy," Michael says, his voice low and almost threatening. "You have no need to panic. I'm not going to hurt you."

I don't answer for fear that anything that I do say will result in him having a meltdown and causing me pain once again. I had gotten away. I had managed to find some solace at Cal's place. A solace that I clearly took for granted. I thought that Michael wouldn't be able to get too close to me at work, but it turns out I was wrong.

"Do you need a drink?" he asks, showing a concern that is laughable after what he has put me through. I shake my head, but he picks a glass up from the bedside table and moves it towards me.

"You really should have some water. You have been asleep for the last fourteen hours."

"What?" I say in surprise before I can stop myself.

"You obviously needed the rest."

He's mental, and I'm fucked.

He brings the glass of water to my lips, and I reluctantly take a sip. It tastes so good against my dry mouth that I quickly devour the lot. Michael chuckles as he puts the empty glass back down.

"See? I knew that you needed a drink. I always know what you need." It's like he's pleased to have some sort of confirmation over a fucking glass of water. He was right. Isn't he always?

"Why am I here, Michael?" I have to ask, even if it does land me in even more trouble with him.

"I'm looking after you."

"But why?" I whisper, pushing myself as far against the head-board as I can. He's so close to me, and it's taking all of my willpower not to grimace.

This man whom I once loved.

This man who once made me feel like a princess.

This man who has become a stranger to me.

"Because I love you." He looks truly perplexed by my question. "You must know that by now?"

"You hurt me, Michael." My eyes well with unshed tears and I look down, trying to keep them at bay.

Michael suddenly grabs my hands, making my eyes fly back up to look at him. My whole body is tense, and my mind is trying to anticipate what he is going to do next. Of course this is a ridiculous thing to anticipate. Michael is unstable, there is no telling what he will do.

"I didn't mean to. I just get a little crazy sometimes, but it's only because I don't want to lose you. I can't be without you, Lucy. You are my life, and I will be damned if anyone other than me is going to spend the rest of their lives with you."

And there we have it. He's never going to let me go.

I don't have the energy to argue with him right now. I have no idea how he got me out of the office at work, or how he got me back to his flat, but I'm tired. I'm tired of fighting and feeling scared.

"I need to get some more sleep," I say, hoping that he will fuck off and leave me alone.

"Of course," he says, granting my silent wish. He stands up and makes his way to the bedroom door.

"Just call if you need anything. I'm not going anywhere," he informs me with a smile before leaving the room and shutting the door behind him.

"Yeah, that's what I'm afraid of," I whisper to myself quietly.

Chapter Fifty-Two

TRYING TO BUILD BRIDGES

The screams echo around the room. The sound of my name being called, urgency in the tone.

"Wake up, baby, please."

A moan escapes my lips, my eyelids flutter, but it's too difficult for me to open them. My head aches, a throbbing pain that has me clutching at it, my fingers curled into my hair. The silent protests of my mind urging the pain to go away.

"Lucy, why can't you just do as I fucking ask? Why must I always have to resort to showing you what will happen if you don't listen?"

Nothing but anger laced in the words being spoken. And fear courses through me, despite the overwhelming pain that I am in.

"Think, Michael."

Michael.

The man who was once my hero.

The man who I thought would love me unconditionally.

The man who has infiltrated every part of my life, making it so damn difficult for me to escape.

"Okay, we're going to have to go out the back way."

He's talking to himself. There is no way that I can answer him. My mouth feels like it is full of cotton wool.

Arms go underneath me, and then I am being lifted. My body rising before my head, the jerk of my neck making me cry out in pain. The sound of him shushing me, holding me close to his body. I feel sick, dizzy, my head dangling down as I struggle to lift it up. He helps me, putting one of his hands at the back of my head and moving it so that it is resting on his shoulder. I feel the strange urge to thank him for this act of kindness. I try to mumble the words, but they don't come out right. He shushes me again and then we're moving.

I have no idea where we are going as all I can think about is blocking out the pain enough so that I don't throw up.

"We won't be long and then I'm going to look after you. I'm going to put all of this right and make sure that no one comes between us again."

I wake with a start, sitting bolt upright in bed, causing a shooting pain to cascade down the right side of my skull. I want to cry out, but I put my hand over my mouth to stifle any noise.

The nightmare that just woke me has left me sweating, my body drenched. It takes me a few moments to calm down as I concentrate on breathing in and out slowly.

I look around the small bedroom and see that I am alone. Breathing a sigh of relief, I prick my ears to listen for any sounds coming from outside the door, but I hear nothing. I want to eradicate the images of Michael hitting me from my mind, but of course, they are ingrained, and I fear that they may never be erased.

The room is dark, and I gingerly move to the edge of the bed, allowing myself to take a moment to allow the slight dizziness in my head to come to a stop. Once the dizziness has subsided, I slowly get to my feet, my legs feeling weak with the effort of standing up.

Taking deep, steady breaths, I move one foot forward, careful not to make any sound. The last thing that I want to do is alert Michael to the fact that I am awake. I need to get out of here, no matter what state I'm in.

Another step taken, another sigh of relief.

I don't have a plan, but my mind focuses on freedom.

I can't stay in this apartment with a man who wants to control my every move.

I can't allow myself to be sucked back in by him.

I never wanted to be this woman. A woman who allowed herself to be abused, mentally and physically. I never imagined that it would happen to me, but then again, no woman would imagine this kind of life as the one that she wants to live.

I make it to the bedroom door, my heart racing, adrenaline pumping through me. I place my hand on the handle of the door and urge myself to be strong.

You can do this, Lucy. You have to get out.

If you don't, he will keep you here, like a prisoner.

With that thought in mind, I push the handle down and open the door a sliver. I peek through the gap and can see that the light is on in the kitchen, but there is still no noise. I open the door some more, my ears pricked. I only open the door enough to squeeze my body through. I put my hand over my mouth to muffle the sound of my heavy breathing, and my eyes stay fixed on the kitchen doorway.

Another step and I'm in the hall.

A couple more and I am stood adjacent to the kitchen doorway on my right, and the front door on my left.

I feel like I want to pass out, but that isn't an option. I can't let this opportunity pass me by. If Michael hasn't heard me already, then there is a good chance that I can get out of here.

A side-step to the left, and then another.

I am inches away from the front door when there is an almighty banging. My back clashes with the wall as I stumble backwards, my heart palpitating with fright.

It takes me a few seconds to register that the banging is coming from the other side of the front door.

"MICHAEL!" an angry voice shouts. "MICHAEL, OPEN THIS FUCKING DOOR!"

Oh my god, it's Cal! Cal's come to get me.

With a renewed batch of adrenaline, I rush to the front door, but before I can lay my hand on the handle, an arm snakes its way around my waist, causing me to jolt, an involuntary shriek coming from my mouth.

"If I were you, I wouldn't do that," Michael sneers in my ear, his lips touching my ear lobe. His tone is menacing, and I know that, at this precise moment, I'm not getting out of here, not by a long shot.

Chapter Fifty-Three

THE CLIMAX

"Michael, I wasn't doing anything." A brazen lie that I know will piss him off unless I can convince him otherwise.

"Don't insult me by fucking lying, Lucy," he sneers, his lips by my ear. The banging on the door continues.

"I'm not lying, I was disorientated and started to panic when I couldn't find you."

"You expect me to believe that?"

"Yes!" I answer urgently. I turn my face to look at him, and I do everything I can to look genuine, even though all I want to do is get away from him. "Michael, you have looked after me, you have been there for me, I see it now, I see how much you have tried to protect me. When I woke up, my head was dizzy, and you weren't there. You promised that you would never leave me, and I woke up all alone—"

"MICHAEL! IF YOU HAVE HURT HER I SWEAR TO GOD THAT I WON'T BE HELD RESPONSIBLE FOR MY ACTIONS!" Cal screams loudly, cutting me off.

Michael is looking at me intently, ignoring the pounding on the door. My heart is beating fiercely as I wait to see if he has bought

180

my bare-faced lies. The seconds tick by, and with each one, I feel my fear building.

"You know, Lucy," Michael starts, his voice low. "You have no idea how long I have waited to hear you say that."

He grabs me and pulls me against his chest, his arms locking around me in a vice grip. I am temporarily stunned by his reaction. I was bracing myself for a punch, not a hug.

"LUCY, CAN YOU HEAR ME?" Cal continues to shout, and I desperately need to see him before he gives up and goes away.

"Michael, you should let me open the door."

"No." His response is instant, his tone firm, but I have to try and convince him.

"I'm not going with him, Michael, but if we don't answer the door then one of the neighbours is going to call the police, and that will open up all sorts of drama that I really don't want to have to deal with."

I have no idea how I am saying all of this off the cuff. I guess my desperation to placate Michael is fuelling my brain to help me voice the words that I need to say.

"I just want to concentrate on us, and I can't do that with Cal trying to smash the door down." I pull my head back and look into Michael's eyes. Eyes which once held so much warmth. Eyes which mesmerised me but now leave me feeling cold inside.

"If I open that door and he so much as dares to come in here, then I won't hold back, Lucy. I won't let him take you from me." His eyes blaze, and I know without a shadow of a doubt that he means every word. His so-called love for me is fucking scary.

"I'm not leaving you, and no-one will take me away." I have to play him at his own game. He thrives on the fear that he instils in me, and I have to try and keep it locked down, hidden away.

"MICHAEL, OPEN THE DAMN DOOR!" More shouts, more time ticking past. Cal must have been shouting and banging for nearly ten minutes by now. More than enough time for someone to have alerted the authorities.

"They better not," Michael replies as he lets go of me. "You stay behind me, and don't talk."

I nod my head and try to contain the bile that is rising in my throat. Michael walks to the door, and I stand there, hoping that I can convey some sort of message to Cal without Michael noticing anything.

Michael grips the handle of the door so hard that his knuckles go white. I hold my breath as the door begins to open and the banging stops.

My eyes connect with Cal's the minute he comes in to sight, and all I want to do is run to him and let him take me somewhere safe. The urge to have him comfort me is overwhelming, but I must compose myself.

If I am to get out of this alive, then I need to trick Michael, just as I did a few minutes ago when I told him that I wanted to be with him.

"You son of a bitch," Cal says before he lunges at Michael. It all happens so quickly.

Cal has Michael pushed against the wall.

Michael has a smirk on his face, and I know that he is formulating a plan.

Cal looks frantic, his eyes locked with Michael's. His hair dishevelled.

I freeze, unsure what to do.

Michael tries to push Cal off.

"Run, Lucy," Cal says, his focus still on Michael.

Run.

That's what I need to do.

An opportunity for freedom.

A lifeline to get away from Michael.

A choice.

If I run, then I'm going to be running forever.

If I stay, then Michael may very well end up killing me.

Two choices, both with shitty endings.

The two men continue to struggle with one another, and I am aware that I need to make my choice before any serious harm can be done.

Run.

Leave.

Get out.

Escape. It's all within my grasp.

Indecision. It clouds my brain.

I don't want to be a coward.

I don't want to drag anyone else into this fucking mess of a relationship.

I need to do this myself. My way.

I have to regain my independence of my own accord.

I can't keep expecting others to save me.

Protect yourself. That's what I should have done in the beginning. And that is what I intend to do now.

Please don't hate me.

Please understand.

"Lucy, come on, get out of here," Cal urges as he chances a look at me. I try to portray how sorry I am without saying anything. Cal knows me, and I have to trust that he will be there for me when this is all over.

Take a chance.

A leap of faith.

I can run, but I can't hide.

I never thought that I would be saying this.

I never dreamed that I would choose this path.

Michael remains quiet, waiting to see what I am about to do, and I am pretty sure that he will also be shocked by my response.

"Lucy, go," Cal urges.

I was ready to stop fighting before, but seeing Cal here, fighting for me, gives me the confidence to know that I can do this.

I'm ready to tackle Michael. I'm ready to take the bastard down.

I'm a fucking fighter, and I hold onto that as I realise my next move could possibly cause irreparable damage between Cal and me.

Forgive me, Cal.

Forgive what I am about to do.

I take a deep breath and open my mouth.

"No."

THE END

Taking Control

What will the consequences of Lucy's actions be?
Part two of the Losing Control series is available NOW!
Taking Control is the conclusion of Lucy's story.

About the Author

Lindsey lives in South West, England, with her partner and two children. She works within a family run business, and she began her writing career in 2013. She finds the time to write in-between working and raising a family.

Lindsey's love of reading inspired her to create her own book series. Her favourite book genre is romance, but her interests span over several genre's including mystery, suspense and crime.
To keep up to date with book news, you can find Lindsey on social media and you can also check out Lindsey's website where you can find all of her books and her newsletter:
https://lindseypowellauthor.wordpress.com

facebook.com/lindseypowellperfect

twitter.com/Lindsey_perfect

instagram.com/lindseypowellperfect

bookbub.com/authors/lindsey-powell

goodreads.com/lpow21

tiktok.com/@lpowperfect

Author Acknowledgements

Thank you to the amazing Melanie who picked another fabulous cover for the start of this duet.

Thank you to my beta readers, Melanie, Nikki and Ashlee. I couldn't do this without the support you ladies give me.

Thank you to my incredible Street Team that share my book posts and teasers. You guys are amazing, and I am always so grateful every time you share.

Thank you to my ARC review team, and to all the new readers that signed up to read this one early.

This book is very different from my usual romantic suspense, but Lucy's story has been with me for a while, and I knew I couldn't just let it sit on my laptop any longer.

As always, thank you to my other half who has to hear me talk all things books 99% of the time.

And thank you to my readers. You are all awesome!

Finally, if you would like to leave a review on amazon, goodreads or bookbub, then just remember, it doesn't have to be a long one, a few words are absolutely fine.

Until next time,

Much love,
Lindsey

Printed in Great Britain
by Amazon

20151117R00113